Robbergirl

S.T. Gibson

Copyright © 2019 S.T. Gibson

All rights reserved.

It is not legal to reproduce, duplicate, or transmit any part of this document in either electronic means or in printed format. Recording of this publication is strictly prohibited and any storage of this document is not allowed unless with written permission from the publisher except for the use of brief quotations in a book review.

This book is a work of fiction. Any resemblance to persons, living or dead, or places, events or locations is purely coincidental.

Eminence Publishing

stgibson.com

ISBN-13: 9781795620031

DEDICATION

To the girls whose names I worshipfully pronounced to myself in secret: you helped make me. To the girls who love hard and loud no matter the consequences: I made this for you.

CONTENTS

Acknowledgments	i
Chapter One	Pg 1
Chapter Two	Pg 12
Chapter Three	Pg 19
Chapter Four	Pg 32
Chapter Five	Pg 42
Chapter Six	Pg 54
Chapter Seven	Pg 65
Chapter Eight	Pg 73
Chapter Nine	Pg 81
Chapter Ten	Pg 110
Chapter Eleven	Pg 122
Chapter Twelve	Pg 133
Chapter Thirteen	Pg 144
Chapter Fourteen	Pg 153
Chapter Fifteen	Pg 172
Chapter Sixteen	Pg 184

ACKNOWLEDGMENTS

I am indebted to my fantastic team of sharp-eyed early readers, McKinley and Joan, who helped me find the vulnerability this book required. Similarly, I would be lost without the inimitable Kit Mayquist, who midwifed this book and played editor throughout the process. Together the three of you kept me focused, attentive to the story, and committed to doing my best work.

I would be remiss not to thank Mr. Hans Christian Andersen, whose source material provided the backbone of this novel. *The Snow Queen* was a beloved companion through most of my childhood, and I hope that this book inspires others to seek it out and enjoy the gifts within its pages.

ONE

Helvig crouched silent and unseen in the branches of a pine tree, an arrow poised between the fingers of one hand and her shortbow gripped in the other. Her thick scarf and cap obscured her face almost completely, except for a sliver of sightline through which she watched the dirt road below.

They had been out here for hours, rooting around for any signs of life on the deserted trade route. The heavy snowfall had deterred most of their usual fare from braving the elements. Merchants weren't often willing to risk getting their wagons stuck in ice, and pleasure travelers were rare this far north even in the most temperate of seasons.

Truth be told, Helvig had expected to spend another uneventful afternoon shivering in the trees, trying to keep up her men's morale while her own mood plummeted with the temperature. She hated looking down the barrel of failure, especially when there was little she could do to change her own luck.

The lifestyle of a thief was decided largely by having the boldness to seize opportunities when they arose, and by having skill enough to escape those opportunities to tell the tale. But no amount of skill could produce unsuspecting travelers where there were none.

A ripple of white caught Helvig's eyes through the trees.

At first, she thought it was one of the animals who grew winter coats to hide themselves in the snow, a hare maybe, or a fox. But then a figure stepped through the forest at the end of the road, and the ripple took the shape of a woman wearing a fine fur cloak. She travelled alone, without so much as a walking stick or scribbled instructions to guide her home. And she was walking in Helvig's direction.

Fortune be praised. An easy target.

The thief hissed down at the three men loitering in the bushes below. It was the sharp, wordless sound mothers used to corral children who squirmed too much in church. Branches cracked and leaves rustled as her men hunkered further down into their hiding places.

Helvig had arranged them in a simple flank formation, so simple even they would be hard-pressed to break rank, and had ordered them to hide until the opportune time.

She prayed they would remember "opportune time" meant once you could see the whites of your quarry's eyes, and not when they were still well down the road with plenty of room to tuck tail and run.

Don't ruin this for us, boys, she thought, and promised herself for the hundredth time that she wouldn't get involved unless absolutely necessary. They would never learn otherwise.

The traveler approached at a meander, face obscured by her hood, hands tucked into a cloak. Helvig sized her up, noting her slight stature and the delicate moccasins she wore, clearly intended for gentler weather. She was no peasant's daughter.

Helvig could practically smell the purse full of family money such a lady must be carrying, and her mouth watered.

She waited until the woman was close enough to see the beaded embroidery on her shoes, and then she strung her bow tight. Her father had taught her the stealth of letting the noises of the forest swallow her own, and the creak of the bowstring blended seamlessly with the groan of trees bending

under the weight of new snow.
   Now, she urged silently. *Act now!*
   Helvig's three men set upon the stranger from the trees and roadside ditches, waving their shining knives at her. They whooped and shouted for her to stay right where she was, but she did not look tempted to run. She simply regarded them quietly from within her hood. Her pale hair hung heavy as hangman's rope over her breasts in two thick plaits, fastened at the end with spherical baubles.
   The crow perched on her shoulder shook the dust from its feathers and gave a mournful cry.
   -kai!
   "Hand over your purses and parcels," Wilhelm growled. Helvig always placed him at the head of the pack because he towered well beyond six feet and had the thick accent of a Bavarian who had not yet acclimated to life in the north. The effect was an intimidating one, and usually enough to make merchants turn out their pockets. He was the oldest of the highwaymen, still young in the face but of the age when men started settling down and siring children.
   The traveler reached up to knuckle the crow under its chin. It wore two cuffs of gold around its tiny feet, and they clinked together when it shuffled on her shoulder. Helvig had never seen a tame crow before, but she tried not to let the oddity distract her.
   Why isn't she screaming or begging for her life? Does she know something we don't?
   "No tricks," Wilhelm said. Behind his back, the two younger boys glanced at each other warily. Helvig could have throttled them. Half of this business was being able to play the part correctly, and they didn't seem interested in committing to their roles.
   The stranger pulled back her hood to reveal blue eyes and a maiden's unlined face.
   Helvig almost lowered her bow. The traveler was no older than she was, just a slip of a girl wrapped in an oversized cloak. She had never seen a woman so young out

on the roads alone. Pity stirred in her chest before she tamped it down.

"I carry neither," the stranger said. Her voice was throaty and weathered, older sounding than Helvig expected.

Wilhelm suppressed a shudder. Someone, somewhere, must have walked over his grave. At least, Helvig hoped that was the case. She couldn't afford him losing his nerve again.

"Don't be clever," Rasmus said. As usual, he wore a nose that had been broken many times and a tattered army coat that had seen more gallant use. The boy always sounded like he was on a stage, but at least he was getting the hang of what to say. Helvig had been his instructor in the fine art of thievery since they were both fifteen, and almost two years later he was still stubborn and slow on the uptake.

The shoulders of the traveler's fox cloak fell back to reveal her collarbones, stark with hunger, and a braid of herbs knotted around her neck. At the end of the necklace hung a small charm inscribed with runes, ancient letters passed down to Swedes and Finns by their ancestors.

"She's a *witch*," Wilhelm hissed.

The word rippled through the highwaymen faster than plague on the back of rats, jumping from one man to the next.

Helvig gritted her teeth. She was losing them.

"Ain't been no witches since the hunts, if there ever were any," a scrawny, pox-faced boy snapped. Jakko was the youngest, all awkward angles and peach fuzz, and he was brandishing a dagger too large for him that was in sore need of sharpening. "Don't go all soft-headed on us."

The German shook his head, making the sign of the cross.

"I knew of a woman in Augsburg. She stole men's potency in dreams and made all the wet nurses in the village dry up. She made charms just like—"

"Did she keep your prick on a tree in her backyard and walk it 'round the town square on a little chain, too? We've all heard the wives' tales, Wilhelm; don't be stupid."

"You grab her then."

Jakko boy blanched and shifted in his boots.

"Why me, eh?"

"She's 100 pounds soaking wet, Jakko," Rasmus said. He looked like he was having great fun despite not being willing to take a step towards the girl himself. He had never been able to resist the siren call of other people's misfortunes, and enjoyed watching them from afar. "Be a man about it!"

Jakko took a faltering step towards the witch, then cast a glance back towards his comrades. Wilhelm motioned him on impatiently.

The boy straightened his back and marched right up to the strange girl. No wavering, just like Helvig had taught him.

"He said give over your purse, girl."

He grasped her tight by the upper arm, and the crow squawked and took flight.

In the space of a breath, she had drawn a gleaming knife from inside her cloak and pressed it to his throat.

Helvig's breath caught, and her arrow strained to fly straight and true, but she didn't fire. Not yet. Jakko had never learned the sense in waiting to act until the last possible moment. He always struck first, convinced everyone was out to get the better of him.

Helvig paused long enough to note that the knife looked like it was better accustomed to slicing apples than slitting throats, and to realize that if the witch wanted Jakko dead, he would be bleeding out in the dirt already.

The girl was bluffing, but only scarcely.

If Helvig had not been the one responsible for keeping Jakko alive, she would have been impressed.

"You will not keep me from my business, boy," the witch said. Her eyes, so placid moments before, had gone storm-dark. "Let me pass."

Helvig spied the tiny tremor in her hand.

Not so accustomed to bloodletting after all, she thought. *But no stranger to rough company, either.*

On the ground, the men grumbled, unsure if coming to

Jakko's aid was the most advantageous thing to do. Helvig watched them deliberate and chewed the inside of her mouth. One less thief alive meant one less slice of the spoils to divvy up, that was true, but you didn't work these roads with a body day in and day out without becoming amicable with them, brotherly even.

Still Rasmus, ever the coward, and Wilhelm, superstitious as a priest, shrank away. Jakko's blood wasn't worth getting cursed by a witch nasty enough to survive the hunts of decades past, it appeared.

Their idiocy was staggering. That girl was no more a witch than Helvig was a saint, but apparently all it took to convince her men was a little rune charm and some unnerving calm.

"I'll gut you," Jakko snarled, and twisted the girl's arm hard enough to bruise. She showed him her teeth.

"Let me go or I'll curse you with the dropsy for the rest of your miserable life."

She was buying time, with no intention of opening his throat right there in front of God and everyone, but the boys were too shaken up to see it.

Jakko spit at her. She started muttering under her breath, dark guttural sounds in a language more fit for the dead than the living.

Wilhelm, who had apparently seen enough of witches in his life to suffer any more, sheathed his knife and began to scuttle away with his hands raised in fearful deference. Chaos swirled among the men, and the sounds of angry, fearsome shouts echoed through the thickly-treed woods.

Helvig groaned.

"That's enough," she said, clear and sharp as a gunshot. "Drop the knife."

The witch looked up and spied the arrow poised over her heart. All the blood drained from her face, and Helvig smiled.

The knife fell from her hand.

Jakko snatched up the knife and shoved the girl away like

she was diseased. Returning the arrow to its quiver, Helvig dropped lightly from the tree. The men parted instinctively, allowing their leader through to the front of the raiding party.

Helvig smacked Rasmus upside his head as she passed.

"You could have done something," she said. "*Anything* would have been nice."

Rasmus glowered at her.

"Wilhelm panicked too!"

Helvig pulled the thick scarf away from her mouth and spat out a long, curling tendril of chestnut hair.

"Then you're bigger fools than I gave you credit for, well done both of you."

She jabbed a threatening finger in Wilhelm's direction but let the issue lie. She would deal with them later.

For now, she approached the stranger in their midst with decisive strides, stopping right in front of her face to show that she wasn't intimidated by her gibberish incantations.

The witch took a half-step back when Helvig encroached, suddenly wary. Pleased at the effect she had, Helvig tilted her head and smiled.

"You must be a very powerful witch, to strike such fear into the hearts of my men," she said, crossing strong arms that were latticed over with the white ghosts of old wounds. Her voice was bawdy-bright and fearless. She had learned her bravado from men twice her size.

"*Your* men?"

They were as close as breath to one another now. Helvig was a little taller and more tanned from summers spent working in the sun, while the other girl was so pale it was almost alarming. Miniscule blue veins showed through her skin.

"Can't you tell? I'm a princess." The archer approximated a crude curtsy. Her upper hand had her feeling braggadocious. "Princess Helvig of the mongrel dogs and God-forsaken bastards, at your service."

Rasmus let out a wheezing cackle, and his laughter was soon joined by the derisive snickers of the other two men.

Helvig's flippancy always emboldened them, even when they were up to their knees in trouble.

"I'm afraid you've fallen in with some of the wickedest company in these woods," Helvig went on. She surveyed the girl's large, deep-set eyes and her lovely thin mouth. As pretty as she was clever, up close. "But what's it to a little finch, winged so far from home?"

"I have business in the north," the witch repeated. She hadn't shrunk away from Helvig outside of that first faltering step, and her voice was steady, but anxiety was building behind her eyes. Her sense of safety was April ice over a frozen lake; false, sheer, and unable to support her weight. How much pressure would it would take to shatter her security? Would the witch cry then? Helvig had never seen anyone keep their head so long during an ambush.

Helvig tugged off her cap, and a mane of tangled curls and knotted braids came tumbling out. She punched a little shape back into her hat and regarded the traveler with a squint.

"There's nothing north of these woods but Samiland and ice. I somehow doubt you've come to do trade with the reindeer herders, since you seem to be in possession of nothing worth selling."

"I seek the queen."

"Sweden has her queen, Charlotte. The north needs no other."

The traveler ran her tongue over cracked lips and cast her gaze from Helvig to the band of thieves and back again.

"I'm looking for the Snow Queen."

Helvig tipped her head back and laughed like a trumpet. The men behind her guffawed and slapped their knees, and she shook her head at them as if to say *pity the girl, she's touched.*

But when she looked back at the cold-eyed girl standing before her unsmiling, uneasiness tapped a little rhythm against Helvig's ribs.

"Come on, birdie," she said. "No need to lie to us. The Snow Queen is a fable. What's your business in these woods?"

"I told you."

"Oh?" Helvig was just as intrigued by this digression as she was irritated. The wise thing to do would be to pat down the girl for her valuables, spook her soundly for good measure, and let her pass unharmed. But Helvig couldn't fathom what circumstances could have possibly led to this chance meeting, and curiosity gnawed at her.

"And what will you do when you find her?"

"I'm going to kill her."

The steel in the girl's voice cut the knees out from any of the men's laughter still rippling in the air.

"Nothing good comes from meddling in the affairs of witches," Wilhelm said warily. Helvig shot him a black look. His superstition had nearly cost them their quarry, and she didn't have the patience for it on a good day.

"We don't even know if she's really a witch, idiot," Jakko said. "She's just some stupid girl pulling fairy stories out of her ass. Snow Queen? Are we really supposed to believe that?"

Helvig couldn't believe that for once, rash Jakko was being the most reasonable out of all of them. Of course, he was right. Wilhelm had called her a witch without her ever having to claim the title, and she only hoped to save her own skin by playing along. Admittedly, it was sly.

"You oughta strip her, Helvig" Rasmus said, scrubbing the frostbitten tip of his crooked nose with the back of his mitten. "See if she's got a witch's teat. That's how they suckle their familiars, you know. I bet that bird of hers is one of the devil's own."

"We could truss her up and throw her in the river," Jakko offered. "See if she floats."

"Nah, I want to see her teat."

"No one's showing their teats," Helvig snapped. She never liked stories about witches. They usually ended with women humiliated and dead.

"We should leave her be," Wilhelm said, from a safe

distance off. "Don't anger her."

Helvig readied herself to lecture the lot of them on how foolish their fears were, but something gave her pause. She knew what would happen if she managed to convince them that there was nothing supernatural about this girl. They would rob the girl and send her on her way, and Helvig would spend the next few days turning her existence over in her head like a riddle that needed solving. It would prick at her, day and night, a secret wound to occupy her mind during the dull stretch of winter.

Something told Helvig she wouldn't be able to forget the color of the girl's eyes either, or the way she kept her hands primly folded even while facing down someone who was in a position to do her harm.

Helvig didn't believe in witches, but she found herself transfixed by this one's unwavering gaze. All of the silver Helvig had stolen over the last fat and spoiled summer felt like dross compared to this girl. She wanted time: to study her, to question her, to admire the slope of her straight nose and swan neck while the boys minded their own business.

Helvig's fingers itched the way they always did when she saw something worth putting her life on the line to steal.

She held out her hand to Jakko and snapped her fingers.

When he passed her the knife he had picked up off the ground, she spun it deftly through her fingers in thought.

If the boys wanted a witch, she would give them a witch. "We'll do this the old-fashioned way," Helvig said.

She grasped the girl by the wrist and pulled her in tightly. She squirmed against Helvig's body, but Helvig cut her off before she could speak.

"Play along," Helvig said quietly, too quietly for her men to overhear. "Don't cry out."

The witch's frightened expression turned wary with intrigue, and Helvig smiled. Then she pricked the girl in the palm with her own knife.

A jolt shook the traveler's body, and blood was briskly drawn. She clamped her lips between her teeth and uttered not a sound, not even when her face turned white as sugar dust on a Linzer tart.

When she opened her mouth to take a shaky breath, a spot of red appeared on her lower lip where her teeth had pierced the skin.

Helvig idly remembered how mother bears nursed their cub's wounds, with a gentle lap of their tongue.

The archer thrust the other woman's palm out towards her men, showing the thin trickle of red that dripped down to stain the snow. Overhead, the crow who had been winging tight circles in the air came to perch in the trees.

-*kai! kai!*

"She feels no pain," Wilhelm hissed. "She bleeds but does not cry!"

"I'll be damned," Jakko said, and whistled lowly for good measure.

Rasmus' face brightened.

"A real witch, just like in the stories! Helvig, if we prod her with a hot poker do you think she'll give us wishes? I heard witch wishes were the best kind."

The witch fixed Helvig with ferocious eyes as her blood pattered gently against the snow. Helvig surveyed the girl's bone-smooth face and the sharp lines of her jaw, cataloguing her features the way she would take inventory of stolen gold.

She squeezed that thin wrist before releasing her, and felt the steady strum of a pulse. Somehow, she was surprised. She imagined a woman so cold and fair to have ice in her veins instead of blood.

"No, Rasmus," she said, never taking her eyes from the witch's face. "She's far too valuable for that. We'll present her properly before the Robber King as a spoil, and he can decide how best to employ her."

TWO

They tied her by the wrists with a mangled piece of twine Rasmus had in his pocket, despite Wilhelm's protestations.

"No rope can hold a witch! She'll slide out of her bindings as soon as our backs are turned and call down the birds to peck out our eyes! It happened to a Berliner I met on the Danish border; I saw the scars!"

"Stop your moaning," Rasmus snapped. "Do you know how lucky we are to have captured a genuine witch? Imagine what life would be like if we could see wealthy merchants coming miles away, or if we had someone to whistle up a storm for us whenever we liked! This is fortune befalling us."

The arguing had continued as they traveled off the path and deeper into the woods, with Jakko occasionally interjecting his inane opinion. Helvig hardly paid attention. She was used to the background din of squabbling men, and she focused on navigating by the dying sun back towards camp.

The girl had stood still for Helvig when she knotted the twine three times around her wrists, and she hadn't winced when Helvig bandaged her bleeding hand with a kerchief filched from Wilhelm. There had been no thrashing and no tears, just the stony set of rage on her features. The girl kept her silence even as Helvig pulled her into the damp of the forest and trekked ahead of her, pushing away fir branches to clear their path.

To tell the truth, it was getting unnerving.

Helvig cast a glance over her shoulder. The three men were dragging behind, with Rasmus regaling Wilhelm and Jakko with his growing list of wishes.

"You put on a fearsome show," Helvig said with casual affect. "But you needn't try so hard to play the part of the heartless devil-wife."

"I don't know what you're talking about," the witch said.

"The boys can't see you from where they are, so you can drop the sorceress act. I'm not so easily frightened."

The girl's eyes flashed with anger. God, she could cut with a look.

"Then why take me for your prize, if my power is of no value to you?"

"Didn't say you were of no value, just said I wasn't frightened of you. I took you because it pleases me to look at you, and because it pleases me to hear you speak. I need no other reason." She tramped through the snow with heavy steps, content to leave the subject there. But it occurred to her that if she wanted to unlock the other girl's secrets, she may have to be a bit more forthcoming about her own. "Although I wasn't fond of the idea of watching the boys subject you to their 'tests' before abandoning you to the weather."

The witch laughed, a sharp bark without any humor.

"A *good Samaritan*! How charming."

Helvig was a bit injured by this. It wasn't every day she stuck her neck out to do the right thing, and she expected a little thanks for it.

"Do you even realize what direction you were heading in? The only thing you'll find at the top of the world at this time of year is a slow death."

"Your opinion holds little weight under the present circumstances."

"Oh? So you really feel nothing, fear nothing?" Helvig had

a spiteful streak, sharpened by a childhood wrestling in the dirt for stolen bread or scheming pranks to get back at bigger children. That streak reared its head now, eager to get a rise out of the unflappable girl. "Not even the Robber King?" Her captive hopped across a fallen log, sure-footed despite the terrain.

"There are things in this world I fear, but a man with a title is not one of them."

"Well, you ought to consider it. He can be fearsome when angry, and has been known to kill strangers on the spot simply for having a suspicious air about them. It's his decision whether you live or die, so you should approach him with courtesy, if nothing else. He'll want to know where you come from."

"My stories aren't his to demand."

"I can tell you're Danish, at least. You speak Swedish like you've got marbles in your mouth."

The witch resumed her unnerving quiet. Helvig felt a fool for trying to make small talk with her prisoner, and hunched her shoulders forward as she continued on her trek.

Thus far, this was not as enjoyable a trip as she had imagined. Maybe she should have just swallowed her pity, sat on her greedy hands, and turned the girl loose when she had the chance.

They walked for a time with nothing but the sounds of the forest settling around them and the chirruping of the crow to break the silence. Then, the witch spoke. Distantly, as if roused from a dream.

"Are you really a princess?"

Helvig looked back at her, a mischievous smirk tugging at her lips.

"Are you really a witch?"

The witch turned her cheek towards her crow, who had been bobbing along on her shoulder through most of their walk. They had been at it for almost twenty minutes now, and the crow didn't look bothered.

"I don't know. Am I a witch, Svíčka?"

-*kai*, Svíčka responded.
"Very clever," Helvig said. "What sort of name is that?"
"Czech. It means little candle."
"Do you have a name as well, or is it only the bird?"
"I'm not in the habit of giving away my name to strangers."
"Well, we're not strangers, are we? Me and the boys gave you our names. That was a gesture of good faith."
The witch snorted in an undignified way that made her nose wrinkle.
"Fine talk from a kidnapping thief."
They came to a brook cutting a dribbling path through a bed of moss, and Helvig leapt over the water as easily as a reindeer. She waited for the witch on the other side with her hand extended, polite as any gentleman helping his lady out of the carriage.
"In my defense, I never robbed you. Don't think I didn't notice that fat little purse weighing down your right pocket, either."
The girl gauged the distance to her captor warily, then reached out with her bound hands to grasp Helvig's fingers.
"If you do not give me a name," Helvig pressed on, "I shall have to gift you one, and be warned, I'm no poet. What's a proper name for a witch, anyway? Knucklebones? Hemlock?"
The witch crossed the brook in one tottering lunge and nearly landed in Helvig's arms. Her long skirts dragged through the water, picking up moss and greenery along the way.
"Gerda," She huffed. "My name is Gerda. I've got no idea what you intend to do with it."
"Call you by it, of course."
"Why, if your men are just going to slit my throat when I refuse to knot winds into rope for them?"
"That, my duck, is your prerogative, and I won't be held accountable for how you choose to conduct yourself among my men. In the meanwhile, I've got manners, so I'll call you

by your name. We're gentlefolk, aren't we?"

"If it's my money you want, you can have it. It isn't worth being delayed like this."

"You were out there wandering blind towards your death. I did you a good turn."

"Why not let me wander towards my death in peace?"

"Are you joking? This is more fun than I've had in ages. Do you know how dull it is, getting sent out with the boys to make sure they don't go pissing on some soldier's campsite?" Helvig puffed out her chest and stiffened her stride as she marched through the forest, dropping her voice to a gravely timbre. *"Get out there with the boys and teach them the ins and the outs, Helvig. They're learning yet, so you'd better not lose any of them. If they get killed, I'll take it out of your cut of the spoils."*

Helvig turned to Gerda, her voice returning to its natural brassiness. "Why is it that I get punished for being good at something, hmm? That oughtn't be the way of things."

The witch blinked vacantly as though Helvig were speaking in another language. The archer sighed, disappointed that her captive had not taken the bait of conspiratorial girl talk. This wasn't going her way at all.

Helvig shouted at the men shoving and chattering some yards off.

"Boys, stop dragging your asses! We're almost home!"

Rasmus jogged to catch up with the girls, wearing a foolish grin. His black hair fell out from underneath his threadbare cap and curled at the nape of his neck like a girl's.

"Say witch, do you keep a black book? The Devil must have given you one when you renounced your baptism and took him for husband." Gerda rolled her eyes, but Rasmus pressed on. "Come on, let's see it! There's no way you can keep all those enchantments between your eyes; you must have them written down somewhere."

"*Tch*," Gerda said derisively, but there was a bit of amusement in her eyes. Rasmus took the inch she gave him and did his damnedest to stretch it into a mile, spreading his arms and walking backwards in front of her like a street urchin hawking wares.

"There were men in the trenches who wore runes round their necks like yours, and I never saw a single one of them die. They fashioned them from pictures in the black books they found in abandoned houses on skirmish lines. They said they saw spells to break fevers, and divinations to determine the outcome of a war. Enchantments, even, to make a man richer than God himself. Oh, miss witch, my kingdom for one peek into your black book!"

Gerda swallowed a smile, and Helvig prickled. Gerda was *her* treasure, and she didn't like the idea of Rasmus swooping in and befriending her in an attempt to win any supernatural favors.

"Are you sure they didn't kick you out of the army for talking too much?" Helvig snapped. "Now turn 'round and walk right; your fool ass is going to fall headlong into a ditch, and I won't cry for you."

"The only thing you've ever cried is piss and vinegar," Rasmus grumbled, but he fell into line all the same.

They were heading down a steep slope now, skittering through birch trees on their way towards a valley clearing. The scent of smoke and slow-roasting meats pricked at Helvig's nose. Judging by the clank of cutlery and clamor of rowdy voices drifting her way, the evening meal had already begun.

Helvig gnawed the inside of her cheek. She would be getting an earful tonight.

"You all keep your mouths shut," she said to her men. Her eyes drifted over to Rasmus. "I'll do the talking for us."

"He's going to be cross with you," Wilhelm sighed, with all the weariness of someone accustomed to giving good advice that was never taken. "He told us to bring back gold, not strangers."

The ground leveled out underneath them as they crossed into the robber's camp.

Helvig thrust Gerda's lead into Wilhelm's hands.

"You let me handle the king. After all." She wiped a bit of

grime from her palms and smoothed her hair. "How can a man refuse the request of his only daughter?"

THREE

The smells of cooking and unwashed men enveloped them as soon as they entered the clearing. Helvig pressed ahead, punching shoulders and shouting hellos as she wove her way towards the center of camp. The boys followed at a more ambling pace, with Gerda trailing behind as far as her lead would allow.

Rasmus ducked into one of the sturdy cold weather huts half-buried in insulating snow, and emerged a moment later gnawing on the remains of a chicken leg.

"Can't wait to see what old Bertie makes of you," he said to Gerda, slurping and smacking his dinner loudly. "It's gonna be a riot."

"He'll probably just have Helvig gut her and steal those embroidered shoes off her feet," Jakko grumbled.

"You'll hold your peace until the King has his say," Helvig shot back.

The camp was not arranged in any particular design, but Helvig had memorized every winding footpath. She remembered her life as a blur of noisy village alleys and roadside shakedowns punctuated by long, sleepy winters dug into remote hideaways. Her father always knew the quietest places to settle in during the cold months when pickings were slim and local constables were bored and eager to sniff out trouble.

She had grown up scraping her knees during forest footraces and dog-piling on top of boys twice her age in the snow, and even though the cast of criminals and runaways who passed seasons under her father's command were in constant rotation, the landscape of woodland and river stayed faithful to her. She could navigate the wide expanse of her father's territory blindfolded and still trust it to lead her home.

Now, she was drawn towards a large bonfire in the middle of camp over which a wild pig rotated on a spit. The ne'er-do-wells were congregated more tightly around the central fire, swapping sips from flasks or cursing their way through tall tales as they warmed their faces on the flames. An old man squatted near the fire, poking at the coals, while two blonde children of grammar school age turned the spit with valiant effort.

Most of her father's company was made up of men, but there were a few women as well, many of whom had shown up at camp attached to exiled husbands or on the run from their own crimes. The thieves were seated on the ground, or on mildewing crates.

One man, however, was seated on a carved wooden trunk with all manner of deerskins and wolf pelts thrown over it. It would not have impressed the king in Stockholm, but it made a fine throne indeed for the ruler of purse-pickers and throat-slitters.

The Robber King had a plaited red beard and a chest like barrel, and he pulled deeply from a churchwarden pipe as he sat with legs spread and boots planted. He was listening to the supplication of two young thieves.

By the look of things, they were squabbling over a golden pocket watch that kept passing between their hands. Eventually, the Robber King plucked up the watch and slid it into the breast pocket of his coat. Like the vest Helvig wore, it had been specially outfitted with all manner of hidden compartments perfect for stowing away contraband.

The Robber King dismissed the two thieves with a jerk of his head. They exchanged crestfallen expressions but did not argue as they slithered back into the crowd.

The King surveyed his realm with the keen agility of an animal on the hunt. When his eyes alighted on Helvig, pressing through the crowd with a fool's smile on her face, they narrowed to slits.

"God's blood girl, don't you think you're cutting it a bit close? Dinner started a half hour ago; I was about to send the dogs out after you."

Helvig bounded to him with breezy nonchalance and clasped her arms around his shoulders. She leaned down to give his bristled cheek a kiss.

"We were busy, papa."

"Busy with thieving, I hope. What did you and the boys bring me? Something better than yesterday's heaping barrels of nothing?"

"Now papa," Helvig began diplomatically.

The Robber King shook his great head, taking Helvig's hands between his own. She had the calloused, nail-bitten hands of a highwayman, but they looked smooth and dainty between her father's.

"My girl, this is the third time this week you've come up empty-handed."

"That's not my fault! The boys—"

"Are your responsibility. And after that cock-up with the silversmith—"

"I conducted myself perfectly! It was Jakko who rushed in and wrestled the gun away from that merchant. He got spooked and shot Rasmus on accident!"

"And whose fault is that? The student's or the teacher's?"

Helvig wanted to defend herself, but she bit her tongue. She would need all the goodwill he had to spare in order to convince him to let her keep her unorthodox prize, and she didn't want to waste it on an argument she had never been able to win.

"Well, I haven't come back with nothing today, papa; quite the opposite."

"Oh? Then I must be going blind in my old age, because I don't see these wonderful spoils anywhere. Have you got a king's ransom of jewels tucked up under your hat? Perhaps you're hiding land deeds in your bodice?"

Helvig was accustomed to his rough teasing, and she saw the love and concern underneath. She popped a boot up on the edge of his throne.

"Answer me this; how did the Finns win their wars when they were so terribly outnumbered? You must recall, you told me the stories so many times I can recite them in my sleep."

The Robber King sighed heavily. He could bluster and chastise all he wanted, but at the end of the day, he was nothing if not indulgent with his daughter.

"They searched field and fen for the most powerful sorcerers they could find. Stationed them along the coast to whistle up winds that would destroy Swedish ships and confuse their sails."

"And so even the smallest nation was able to make the great northern empire tremble! Imagine what men of fortune could do with the powers of magic on their side. We could enchant horses to throw their riders, summon a thick mist to disorient merchants while we ambushed, hypnotize wealthy ladies and snatch the diamonds right off their bosoms!"

She was weaving her own kind of spell with words, caught up in the act of creation. Her father merely blinked at her behind knit eyebrows.

"Where is this going, Helvig?"

Helvig swept her arm towards Gerda as though she were introducing a young lady into high society.

Wilhelm nudged Gerda gently forward, and the pale girl approached the king with a bird-like wariness in her eyes. Some of her flaxen hair had been pulled free from her plaits by the snag of branches, and the hem of her dress was filthy, but Helvig still thought she looked every inch a sorceress—as beautiful and terrible as a bedtime story.

"I have brought you a powerful witch, papa," she continued. "I snared her on the roadside as she was out and about her dark business. Mind that charm round her neck; she knows the old language and is cunning in the ways of heathenry."

A small, curious crowd had gathered to give Gerda a once-over, muttering between themselves. But despite the drama being played out in the center of camp, the bustle of everyday life continued undeterred. This was unsurprising. Helvig had never known all the men to stand at attention for any occurrence, except perhaps the time some of the night girls from Gothenburg paid their camp a visit.

The Robber King stroked his beard in thought, surveying Gerda from toe to crown. Helvig didn't dare speak while her father deliberated. His word was the only law the brigands obeyed, and he would not be rushed in his deliberations.

The King poked a thick finger at Svíčka.

"What's that bird there on her shoulder?"

Helvig thought on her feet. Rasmus wasn't the only one who could spin a tale quick as a whip.

"It's her familiar, father. A bit of the devil's own soul left to guard her and guide her in the ways of magic."

"And that twine round her wrist?"

"We couldn't have her running off, and who knows what kind of dark incantations she can weave with those fingers?"

"She's too thin. Does she eat?"

"Well, the succor of sin saps the strength from anyone."

He nodded at Gerda's bandaged hand, and the thin smear of blood that had dried along her wrist. Helvig hadn't cut her very deeply, but she hadn't scrimped on the blood she'd drawn either.

"Damaged?"

"That's my fault, I'm afraid. I had to put her to the test to be sure of her authenticity."

The Robber King took a long draw from his pipe. Then he handed it to his daughter and beckoned Gerda closer.

"Come here, enchantress. Let me look at you."

Helvig stepped behind her father to watch the proceedings with her knuckles pressed to her mouth. She didn't have his approval yet, but she had his attention, and that was half the battle.

When Gerda didn't move, she jerked her chin towards the ground and mouthed *kneel!*

Gerda took a few steps forward and sank onto the soggy ground with a grace Helvig had only ever imagined the nobility possessed.

"Do you traffic with the Devil, girl?" Helvig's father asked sternly. He had raised his voice for the benefit of the onlookers. "Have you suckled at his breast or written your name in his book?"

Gerda cast a wary glance to Helvig, who widened her eyes and raised her eyebrows. She could only do so much for Gerda if the witch wasn't willing to play along, and if Gerda wanted to call this whole thing off by confessing to her deception, this was her chance.

Helvig doubted she would, however. Her alleged powers were the only thing keeping her from getting robbed blind.

"I have met devils aplenty on my journeys through the dark of the woods." Gerda's voice had taken on the same eerie formality she had used when addressing the men who attacked her, a hint of something ancient threaded through her words. "Some took the forms of animals or humans, others spoke to me out of the ether and the trees."

"And what are their names, these devils?"

"I cannot say."

The Robber King leaned back in his seat and made a grunt that came from deep in his chest. He beckoned to Helvig and she leaned in, her arms folded across her chest.

"Are you pulling my leg?" He asked quietly.

"What? No!" Helvig dropped her voice to a vehement whisper and leaned in even closer, cheeks burning with embarrassment. "She's a witch, and a useful one! Moreover, you can't prove that she isn't."

"I don't have time for any of your nonsense. What am I supposed to do with her? What will she eat; where will she stay?"

"With me, of course!"

"We have our rules, Helvig. A body works, a body eats, simple as that. Everyone here has got to have a skill; if they aren't thieving, they need to be pulling their weight tending to the horses or keeping the blades sharp."

"When she's not witching, she can cook or darn socks or—"

"Your Majesty?"

The faces of the royal family snapped over to the interloper. It was not the young witch still kneeling on the ground, but Jakko instead. He stood with his hat clutched in his hands.

"Yes?" The Robber King asked.

Jakko gestured to Gerda as though showing off his finest mare. "I'd like to lay a claim on the girl, seeing as it was I who first stole her. It's within my rights, Your Majesty."

Helvig was so furious she saw spots.

"You didn't find her; I found her! I spotted her first and I carted her home!"

"Well I grabbed her, so she's mine."

Helvig passed her father's pipe back and marched up to Jakko, practically fuming smoke from the ears. Her father's interrogations she had expected, but she wouldn't tolerate being publicly challenged by some twelve-year-old upstart who thought taking what other people had rightfully stolen made him a man.

"You can't call grabsies when you stood there pissing your pants from fright when she threatened to turn you into a toad."

Jakko threw his hat on the ground, all pretenses at civility lost.

"You're a liar!"

"What would you even do with something so pretty and powerful, stupid boy? You just want to steal her because you

can't find a sweetheart who will put up with your horseshit."
"Neither can you, ugly goblin," Jakko said with a sneer.
Helvig boxed his ears, and he took a swipe at her. This was the last straw for Helvig, and the anger bubbling up in her chest erupted as she slapped him across his smug face.

It felt good, to hit back. Violence had nursed and raised her, and she never had a more trustworthy companion than the strength of her own fists.

Jakko lunged on her and in an instant they were tussling in the dirt.

The Robber King looked on patiently, puffing on his pipe. Some of the men who had gathered to watch Gerda's presentation lost interest and wandered off to find entertainment they hadn't seen a hundred times before. Others hollered out obscene encouragements, or swapped money for bets. Helvig hardly noticed. She was too busy bruising Jakko's ribs with her knees and batting away the fingers clawing at her face.

Jakko fought dirty, letting out a string of curses as he swung wide with his bony elbows. He had joined the camp six months ago as a nasty little boy with blood on his hands and had only gotten crueler with age and experience. But she was still bigger, and would be for a few years yet.

He tried to pull out a fistful of her hair and she socked him in the nose, hard. He raked his nails across her cheek but by this point, Helvig had managed to wrestle atop Jakko. She pinned him down with an elbow to his shoulder and bit him on one of his unwashed ears. The boy gave a yelp and scuttled out from underneath her. His nose was bleeding freely.

Chastened for a time, Jakko pressed through the small crowd of onlookers with his ear throbbing red. Helvig pulled herself to her feet and straightened her vest, spitting on the ground where Jakko had just lay. She could taste blood on her mouth: his, from his new wound, and hers, from the lip he had split open with a fist.

Helvig locked eyes with Gerda, still kneeling mere feet

away with an ashen face. Her formal mask had slipped, and there was shock in her eyes, perhaps fear as well.

Helvig reddened with embarrassment, and she smudged the blood off her lip with what she hoped was a dainty gesture.

Jakko's curses echoed distantly for a moment as he fled, and then all was calm once again.

"Apologies, my king," Helvig said once she had caught her breath. Adrenaline and jealousy still buzzed like bees in her stomach. "But as you can see my prize is just as valuable as silver or gold. I beg you to welcome her into camp. She is an ally, and a powerful one at that."

"And how am I supposed to know this slim-hipped little 'ally' of yours isn't going to steal the horses while we sleep?"

"If she gets a funny look in her eye, I'll tickle her with my knife. I'll keep her in line, Father, I swear it."

The Robber King kneaded his brow with a mammoth hand.

"Since you found her, she's your responsibility. Just like that stinking deer of yours."

Helvig's heart leapt with hope.

"And isn't Bae well behaved? Haven't I taken such fine care of him?"

"Keep your witch on a short leash. I don't want her giving the men any heartsickness or brackening our drinking water. And if she can't pull her weight, she's out on her ass Helvig, end of story."

Bored now that the King had passed his ruling, the men who had gathered began to mill about once more. Some of them mumbled about the princess' strange taste in friends, or about witches having found their winter hideaway, but Helvig clapped her hands together for joy and beamed at Gerda.

"Hear that? Now thank the King for his graciousness."

"Thank you," Gerda said, and rose to her feet.

"Wilhelm, go find the witch something to eat," The Robber King said. "She looks like she's about to keel over. You can untie her, and if she causes any trouble for you just dunk her in the river to straighten her out. Helvig, a word if you please."

He gestured for her sit on a fur by his feet. Despite how much she wanted to bound after Gerda and congratulate her for impressing the king, Helvig happily obliged. She had warmed herself by the fire at her father's feet since she was a tiny child. It was a sacred place where she had always been well-protected and well-advised.

The Robber King propped his elbow on his knee, leaned in close, and squinted an eye at her.

"I may be an old man, but I'm not as stupid as these boys. That girl is not a witch."

Helvig took a gulp of air. A fool's optimism seemed like the best choice in this situation.

"Maybe not. But she *could* be."

"If you wanted a friend so badly, I could have just found you one."

The tips of Helvig's ears flared red, and she glowered at the ground. She had never been able to bluff him, not even for an instant. He had taught her better than to take people at face value, and she should have known he would not be so easily beguiled by Gerda's runes and unnerving eyes.

"I wanted her. Is that so terrible? It's boring here all winter when no one new arrives and we've got nothing to do but hunt and gamble and argue. She was interesting, so I took her. I thought that was allowed."

Her father took one last puff of his pipe, then tapped out the ash on the ground and began to clean the bowl with his shirttail.

"Listen you me. There are no saints among us. We cheat and pillage and profit off the misfortune of others, and sometimes we spill a little blood to win the day. But we aren't kidnappers. Why don't we kidnap people, Helvig?"

"Because kidnapping invites retaliation," The Robber Princess grumbled.

"What happens when one of the nearby villages come looking for their lost daughter with torches and pistols? Then we have to scatter again, and there goes our plan of passing a quiet winter working these roads. Her clothes are too fine for her not to belong to anyone."

"There isn't a town anywhere around, just deer paths and trade routes. She isn't out here because she's lost."

"In that case she's walking the borderlands in December because she *wants* to, and that should give you even more pause."

Helvig's heart, so full only moments before, felt like it was being drained in a winepress.

"She said she was heading north, chasing some fairy story. It's miles from here to the nearest Sami village; she would have died out there, papa. It made me sick to think of her freezing to death."

"That's her prerogative. Maybe her business really is witching or maybe it's something you want nothing to do with. She may look harmless, but the worst devil is the one you've never met before."

Helvig scuffed at the ground with the heel of her boot.

"Do I have to take her back, then?"

The Robber King leaned back in his seat, releasing Helvig from the grip of his undivided attention. "Not after the show you've made of things, turning her out like a Rus *tsarina* for all the men to marvel out. She's your charge now so you mind her. But if I were you, I would sleep with one eye open. That one is smart, and she's not keen on passing a winter here with us, I can see that much."

"I'll convince her," Helvig declared. It couldn't be that hard to win over another girl. Age and nature would make easy friends of them.

"You can try. But I'll remind you that tying people up and stabbing them is no way to win allies. Was that really necessary?"

"I wanted the boys to believe she was dangerous so they would keep away and give us some peace and quiet."

The King made his rumbling thoughtful sound again.

"You've always had a thief's appetite for the world,

Helvig. Stuffing your pockets with every beautiful thing you can find without asking who it belongs to or where it's come from. But people are not baubles to pluck up as you please. They require finer finesse."

Helvig continued to wear a furrow in the ground with her boot, brooding loudly without having to say a word.

Her father drew a deep breath and then cleared his throat. He had a reputation for laughing in the face of fear and had once finished a card game with a piece of shattered liquor bottle sticking out of his leg after a tussle with a disgruntled tavern-goer. But now, he looked a bit trepidatious.

"Listen to me, Helvig. I understand how important it is for a growing girl to have, well…a companion, of her own age. Someone to share her interests and celebrate her successes. I am sorely sorry that pickings are so slim among the castoffs of genteel society. So I don't begrudge you feeling the need to rope a girl out on the road and carry her home as plunder. But that…isn't how most young ladies make the acquaintances of other young ladies."

Helvig smiled wickedly.

"Ah, but I'm not a lady. I am a princess, and princesses should always have their way, and I am a thief, and thieves always take what they want. Just like you took me."

The Robber King let out a laugh and squeezed Helvig's shoulder.

"You've always been sharp, my little brigand. You would do so well in the city with a proper education. I wonder some days if I'm doing you a disservice bringing you up so far from society and its charms."

Helvig leaned her chin against her father's hand. The warmth from the fire was making her eyelids heavy, and his presence brought her more comfort than wine or gold.

"Hang society. I would rather sleep with the reindeer every night and eat nothing but pinecones and roots if I didn't have to answer to anyone. You've done a fine job raising me."

The Robber King ran a thumb over Helvig's cheek, then looked over to Gerda, who was lingering near one of the larger fires with a piece of brown bread held between her hands. She was dipping it into a pot of rabbit stew and smiling wryly between bites at Rasmus, who was engrossed in telling one of his tall tales.

"Any girl who can survive on her own out here and keep her head is hardy indeed, and a fine friend for my daughter."

"You see why I wanted her."

"Perhaps. Perhaps she will decide to make camp with us of her own volition, at least for a little while." Gravity settled over his features. "But if she decides to leave, you can't keep her here. Do you understand?"

Helvig watched Gerda scoop the last bit of broth from her bowl and suck the final drop from her fingers. A terrible pang went through the Robber Princess's chest.

"I s'pose."

"Go tend to your witch. God knows she's got a chill enough look in her eye to play the part. And you let the men think what they want to think about that; it might keep them from haranguing her too much. Pretty girls breed trouble."

"She is pretty, isn't she?" Helvig mused, watching the way the firelight gleamed through Gerda's impossibly long hair, swinging like a veil down to her hips. Helvig had never seen a woman with hair so perfectly kept, except in the ballet advertisements she sometimes found on the road and kept tucked under her bed. Sonja their smithy kept her hair cropped by her ears, and Helvig cut the matts out of hers with a knife when they became too unmanageable.

Her father squinted sidelong at her.

"Go on, now. And mind what I said about trouble."

FOUR

When Helvig slipped into the circle of light cast by the fire and sat herself down by Gerda on a fallen tree, Rasmus was pantomiming a rapier fight
"He thought he could get one over on me, but I saw the rakish look in his eyes and I knew the villain wasn't going to fight fair. So, I parried and thrust and took a swipe at him with my leg—" Rasmus acted out his victory with great gusto, and Wilhelm chuckled around his tankard. "And down he fell, flat on his back! I stood over him with my sword to his throat and I made him apologize for all those things he had been so bold to say when he thought I couldn't hear him. He was practically kissing my boots when it was all over."
"Finely done," Gerda said. Rasmus bowed low to her and she gave an indulgent smile and a brisk clap, elegant but restrained. It appeared she wasn't so afraid of him when there weren't knives being waved around.
"I see you've become acquainted with our prince of tall tales," Helvig said, stabbing with a wooden spoon at the congealing stew hanging over the fire. She had brought over a bit of meat from the pig roasting over by her father.
Rasmus leaned on the stick he had been using in lieu of a sword.
"But this story really did happen, Helvig."

"Did it?" Wilhelm said with a laugh. The huge man was seated on the ground with his back against Gerda's log. "All just as you've said?"

"Well...there's no accounting for a little artistic embellishment to sweeten a tale's telling."

"No, of course not," the German said, and winked sidelong at Gerda. Helvig pursed her lips together as she spooned herself a heaping bowl of stew. She felt as though all her men had gotten quite friendly with her prize while she had her back turned, and she hoped they remembered that Gerda was her guest, not theirs.

"Let him lie," Jakko said wearily, drawing a tattered blanket tighter around his shoulders. His ear had stopped bleeding, but he still refused to meet Helvig's eyes. "We need something to keep us entertained out here in this wretched place."

"If you don't like it you can march your ass back to Jämtland and see how well they receive you," Helvig shot back. She was feeling testy after their scuffle, and watching Rasmus preen and flex for Gerda hadn't helped her mood.

"Jakko's right," Gerda said. Her voice made even the most mundane observation sound like a divine pronouncement.

Helvig was so taken aback that her spoon stopped halfway to her mouth, hovering in midair. It was a strange thing for anyone to take Jakko's side, much less an outsider who had been terrorized by him hours before.

"Stories make living tolerable for even the most wretched creatures," the witch continued, tucking a few breadcrumbs away in her pockets. For her devil-bird, Helvig supposed. She didn't see it anywhere so it must have found a dark place to roost through the night.

"You're going to defend him?" Helvig said. "After the way he tried to barter for you like a milking cow?"

"You've railed on him enough today," Wilhelm said, giving Helvig one of his convicting blue-eyed looks. "The scriptures say we ought not let the sun set on our anger."

Jakko sniffed self-righteously.

"That's right."

"As if you care about some dusty old book," Helvig sneered.

"I care about plenty of things when they serve me."

"Speaking of the word of God," Rasmus broke in, tired of their sparring. "What did your father have to say to you? Is he angry we didn't make our quota again?"

"I don't understand the point of his impossible demands," Jakko groaned. "It's almost Christmastide; the trade routes are dry."

"My father expects much of us, but he isn't unfair," Helvig said, declining to share the gentle chastisement she had received moments ago. "Failure is an excellent teacher, and you lot need remedial lessons."

"Are you all thieves?" Gerda asked, as politely as if she were asking a suitor what he did to earn his living. Helvig was once again staggered by her breezy affect, but it occurred to her that this was perhaps how Gerda survived on her own, by keeping her courtesies about her at all times. It certainly prevented anyone from seeing deeper into her mind, into whatever schemes or fears might be rooted there.

"Most of us steal to earn our place here," Helvig supplied. "Others have valuable skills we can't afford to bounce from township to township looking for. Better to keep a low profile and welcome those who come seeking solace outside the bounds of society"

Helvig offered Gerda some of her roasted pork, hoping to foster a bit of goodwill. The witch smiled but shook her head, not quite meeting Helvig's eyes. She couldn't tell if Gerda was angry with her or just being polite.

"Do you ever go into the towns?" Gerda asked, taking in her host with a quick flick of her eyes.

"Of course. We send men out to buy supplies, and sometimes the boys and I sneak into villages for a draught or a seat at the tavern shows".

"Helvig lives for the dancing girls," Rasmus said with a roll of his eyes.

Helvig bristled. She felt like Rasmus was teasing at a secret, flashing a glint of it the way a rich man might flash his pocket watch to show off his station. She didn't like it.

"And why shouldn't I? I don't expect your walnut brain to appreciate high art."

"That's all well and good," Jakko cut in. "But what about our witch? Can we keep her or not?"

Helvig looked to Gerda, her eyes lingering for a moment on her mouth. The memory of swaying wheat and the sour taste of strawberries rippled through her mind before vanishing.

"I can keep her, if she'll deign to be kept."

Her father's urgings returned to her, cooling the fire in her blood. She couldn't force a friendship here. But she could strongly suggest it

"I don't wish to call down your ire on our camp for holding you against your will," Helvig said. "But the northern roads are treacherous this time of year. Won't you pass a few more nights with us around the fire?"

"Your father certainly seems to think I should," the witch said smoothly, legs crossed. Her body was angled away from Helvig, her face that same unreadable mask. "I've always been taught it's rude to refuse a host's hospitality, especially when that host is only keeping you alive to indulge a spoiled girl's whims."

Helvig dropped her spoon into her bowl.

Around her, the boys exchanged looks of horrified delight at this flagrant trespass. Everyone knew that if the Robber King overheard someone talking poorly of his daughter, he had them strung upside down from a tree so she so could stand beneath them and accept their blubbering apology. If Helvig overheard you...well, there was at least one bruised rib and black eye guaranteed, even if she had to drag over a stepstool to reach your face.

Rasmus held up two fingers to indicate his bet, and Jakko nodded surreptitiously and flashed three with a jerk of his chin to Gerda.

Helvig ground her teeth for a moment, then gave a nod. Finesse, her father had said. She must use finesse. When she spoke, her voice was measured.

"You're cross with me. I understand."

Rasmus' jaw dropped. Jakko snickered and pranced around the fire to collect his dark horse prize. Helvig pretended not to see them exchanging coins and continued.

"Maybe it was a bit excessive to tie you up—"

"You *stabbed* me," Gerda huffed, a bit of genuine hurt slipping into her voice. A long day of keeping up her impassibility must have finally gotten to her. "If charity was what you had in mind, you could have been gentler."

"And maybe I should have presented coming back with us to camp as more of a...recommended option—"

"And insult my intelligence with a lie? You would be worse off than you are now."

Helvig was losing her patience. She wasn't used to being gracious, and she hated being made to look bad in front of the boys.

"Listen girl, I saved your life. You might not be able to see it now, but come the dark days you'll be thanking me. You won't want to be caught north of this encampment in a few weeks' time. There are worse things out there than hunger and cold."

This sobered up the party of brigands considerably. Gerda just stared expressionlessly into the fire, the icy walls that surrounded her standing at attention once again.

After a disquieting silence she said,

"Perhaps."

"Well," Wilhelm said awkwardly, stretching out his long limbs. "I'm tried. Goodnight, Princess. Miss witch, *gute Nacht*."

"To bed with you, then," Rasmus said, sitting himself down cozily close to Gerda on the log. He took the seat right up next to her at the end, leaving Helvig alone a few feet away on the other side. "Now where will our esteemed guest be sleeping this evening? You're free to bunk with me.

Whisper your arcane secrets into my ear and I shall warm you well indeed."

Despite the fact that she had both extended and received much coarser propositions in her day, Helvig flushed like a schoolgirl. She considered giving Rasmus a lecture at knifepoint on the finer points of civil discourse, but Gerda was unphased. She smiled smoothly, betraying no sentiment.

"You would find me a dull bedfellow, dear soldier, as I am sworn to secrecy on matters esoteric and otherwise immune to the charms of men."

"Perhaps it's I that's been charmed, then. I shall waste away this night tortured by evil visions of you."

"Even a witch cannot be held responsible for the dreams of men."

Rasmus clutched his heart as though pierced and let out a moan of defeat. Jakko laughed, some light leaping into his beady eyes. Helvig had rarely seen him smile like this, wide and gap-toothed without any whisper of cruelty.

"It's a rare woman who can talk circles around our Rasmus," Jakko said. "I'll drink to that."

Wilhelm raised his tankard in approval and drained it to the last as Helvig stood and brushed the day's filth from her breeches. The proper thing to do in this situation was to extend the hospitality of her own warm bed, especially considering that her guest was a young lady just like she was. It would be expected. Perfectly seemly.

But when Helvig spoke, her mouth was as dry as it was when she bet her entire day's score at the card tables.

"Come on, witch. You can sleep with me, away from these scabs."

Gerda patted Rasmus' hand and rose from her seat in a sweep of lichen-colored linen.

"Better luck with a sweeter maiden," she said.

Rasmus tipped his hat back and crossed his arms. He was regarding Helvig levelly, as though counting off paces before turning to shoot.

"Suit yourselves. Warm her well, Princess."

Helvig bit back a heated reply. As much as Rasmus liked to irk her, he should have known better. Some wounds never healed well enough to weather mockery.

Part of her, indignant, wanted to drag Rasmus into the woods for a talking-to. Another part of her, fueled by shame, wanted nothing less than to draw any more attention to her inappropriately sized feelings.

In the end, shame won out.

"Goodnight, then," she said tightly, and disappeared into the chill dark.

Turning back to see if Gerda was still following would be too embarrassing by far, but she could hear her light steps in the snow. Helvig deliberated whether or not to go straight to bed, then banked sharply right and ducked beneath some low fir trees at the edge of the forest.

Helvig pushed back the branches and made a clicking sound with her tongue. The crunch of snow beneath hooves greeted her, and she cooed with delight when Bae poked his muzzle out of the trees.

No matter what mood she ended the day in, a quick visit with her beloved reindeer always lifted her spirits. Checking on him before bed was as much a part of her routine as pulling on her leathers in the morning before hitting the roads, or circling around a fire at night to share dinner with her father's men.

She clasped her arms around Bae's neck and nuzzled his shiny fur. The stress of the day melted away as Helvig breathed in his spicy musk and synced her lungs to his breathing. She and the reindeer had been inseparable since the moment she first clambered up onto his back, took fistfuls of his fur in her tiny hands, and begged her father to buy him for her.

"You ready for bed, smelly?" She asked, scratching the white fur under his chin. "It's been such a long day, hasn't it?"

Behind her, Gerda shifted closer, and Helvig turned to find her gazing at the reindeer with something close to wonder. Her eyes had softened now, not so much the otherworldly blue of fairy lights, but more the pale cornflower of a child marveling at a tree hung with Christmas candles.

"Have you never seen a reindeer before?" Helvig asked.

"Not this close. He seems so tame."

"That's 'cos he's a big scaredy-cat. I still wouldn't get behind him; he's a kicker. But he's never bitten anyone, far as I know. Never tried to run, either. We keep him tied up mostly out of habit."

Bae tossed his head, and the bells hung from his bridle sang a merry tune. The bridle was woven from cords of bright red and white, in a pattern distinctive to one of the prominent reindeer herding families of the north.

"Is he a Sami deer?" Gerda asked. She shuffled silently closer, her face rapt with adoration. She was even more beautiful like this, when she didn't veil her emotions behind formality. Helvig would never have guessed that a girl who seemed carved from ice would melt over something as silly as a common deer.

"That's right. Or he was, before my father gifted him to me. Now he's fat and spoiled and never has to do any work. Isn't that right, shithead?"

Helvig continued to insult the deer in a doting voice and scratch him behind the ears. Gerda was a mere foot away now, entranced by Bae's velvety antlers and soft suede eyes.

Bae gave a wet snort and the witch started. Helvig chuckled, then reached out to take Gerda's gloved hand in her own. Pulling off the glove by the fingertips, she gently led Gerda's palm to press against Bae's snout.

A smile broke across Gerda's face; midnight sun in a world of darkness.

"What do you think?" Helvig asked. She was close enough to feel Gerda's warmth. Their shoulders touched beneath heavy winter coats, and the thief's breath stirred the flyaway hairs at Gerda's temple.

Gerda tugged off her other glove and brought both hands up to cradle Bae's face. His huge lashes swept docilely over his eyes as she ran her fingers across his nose and ears.

"He's amazing. Such a beautiful animal."

"Hear that, smelly boy? You have her fooled. You've bewitched the witch."

A ruffle of feathers overhead caught Gerda's eye, and she smiled up to her crow, perched in the boughs above the heap of straw and dry grasses where Bae made his bed.

"There you are, Svíčka. Are you sleeping with Bae tonight?"

The crow blinked drowsily before tucking its head back into its feathers.

"I'll be damned," Helvig said. "Our animals are conspiring together."

"A powerful political allyship," Gerda said with a smile.

She gave a dreamy sigh and snuggled her cheek against Bae's neck. Helvig hadn't realized how tightly wound the other girl was, how she held tension in every muscle of her body, until she relaxed against the animal's warmth. Now, in the quiet of the wood with Gerda's eyes half-closed in sleepy delight, Helvig felt like she could ask her anything, like they could become conspirators too.

"How did you come across such a well-trained bird, at any rate?"

Gerda yawned, kissed Bae on his nose, and began to pull on her gloves. When she spoke, the shimmering softness in her voice had faded, replaced by hollow civility.

"Our animals have got the right idea. We should sleep if we want to catch any of the light tomorrow morning."

Helvig's shoulders sagged. Perhaps she had ruined her chances for friendship when she had aimed an arrow at Gerda's heart, or when she had pricked her in the palm. Or perhaps Gerda was not the kind of girl who would allow herself to be made friends with.

Helvig had never known a creature so guarded. Even a newborn deer would eat out of your hand if you were still and patient for long enough.

"You're right," she said, a little roughly. "Off we go,

then."

    Helvig gave Bae one last pat and then began to tramp through the snow towards her tent. She did not look back for Gerda.

FIVE

Gerda moved like a shade through the trees, a barely opaque impression of a girl that may slip out of existence at any moment. Helvig thought it must have been the inconstant firelight outdoors that gave her such an otherworldly cast, but when Gerda stepped into the yellow glow of the robber's tent, her alien fairness stood out all the starker.

Helvig's tent was built up with wooden slats and packed in with snow, well-protected against the biting cold but hardly big enough for one person to stand up in without stooping. The girls moved past each other in an awkward rustle of leather and skirts as Helvig shut the tent flap behind them.

Gerda cast her eyes over Helvig's makeshift bed of blankets and furs, her meager trunk of road-battered clothes, and her reindeer bridle tossed haplessly in the corner. Helvig had never realized until that moment how few fine possessions she had; just half a bottle of Italian wine swiped off a missionary and one good pair of dancing boots, laced up with red Sami ribbons. She pawned most of what she stole after turning the king's cut in to her father, or traded it for food, clothes, or supplies. In this life there was no point being weighed down by possessions that didn't keep you alive or make you stronger. The only spoil she had kept for herself was a garnet drop earring she had asked Wilhelm to stab into her ear with his strong hands. Even she wasn't immune to a little vanity.

Now, she was overtaken with the urge to shove Gerda out of the tent and not let her back in until she had cleaned the interior from top to bottom. For all Helvig knew, the witch could be accustomed to luxurious surroundings, and Helvig was embarrassed to show off a home so poor and untidy.

Helvig usually couldn't care less what people thought of her or her home, but there was something about Gerda that had her scrambling to impress.

"The accommodations are a bit sparse," Helvig said.

"On the contrary, I think I'll be quite comfortable."

Helvig had no idea what to do with her hands, so she plopped down on the frayed rug thrown over the dirt and began to fastidiously unlace her boots. There was something about Gerda's closeness in her private space that made it hard to meet the other girl's eyes.

"Sorry about the boys. They wouldn't know manners if it bit them in the ass."

Gerda lowered herself gingerly onto the edge of the trunk where Helvig stuffed her clothes. She did not look necessarily at ease, but rather like someone who was making her very best effort to *seem* at ease.

"I've made civil conversation partners out of worse people. They seem harmless enough, underneath all the bluster."

"Idiots, all of them. But well-meaning ones."

"You're very hard on them," Gerda said. Not an accusation, just an observation.

"Well, it's like training a pup. Have to make it respect you before it'll be sweet on you."

"And which one of them are you hoping will turn out sweet on you?"

Helvig was almost strangled with mortification.

"Oh no, I didn't mean—Any of them? Oh no! Jakko's an absolute ass who ran somebody's brother through with a sword and now he can never show his face in polite society again. Never learned to keep that temper in check." She was tripping headlong over her words in attempt to regain control, her battering heart urging her to *stop talking*. Gerda seemed to be taking a small, private pleasure from the way Helvig flushed, and Gerda's growing smile disoriented the thief even more. "And well, Rasmus is about as fearsome as a soldier made of tin. A deserter, you see; hardly lasted a week on the front lines. He's so thick in the head that I still have to take him out thieving with me and keep an eye on him even though he's been with us for years."

"What about Wilhelm?"

"Wilhelm is a Catholic and father says there's nothing wrong with that, but you know how they are. Superstitious, moralizing. He lived on a border town between papist Rhineland and the Lutheran North, and when the Lutherans came calling Wilhelm didn't bend. So, down burns his house and off his children and wife get carted for re-education and the next thing he knows he's on the run."

Gerda made a hum of knowing, locking these tidbits of information away for later use at her discretion. Helvig couldn't believe how little it had taken to get her to sing like a finch. Just one sweet smile and the gentle suggestion of romantic entanglements and she had handed over her men's histories.

She knew the witch had a strange and powerful effect on her—she wouldn't have stolen her otherwise—but this was alarming. Helvig, who fancied herself a chivalrous and magnanimous host, was supposed to be the one in charge here, not Gerda.

"Robbery doesn't seem like a likely profession for a man so pious," Gerda mused.

"Robbery is a likely profession for any man with an empty belly. His piety doesn't stop him from swindling and cheating, it just makes him miserable about the whole thing. And no fun to be around on Sundays."

Gerda shifted her cloak off her shoulders and began to

fold it neatly. She wiggled out of her filthy moccasins, revealing tiny feet with soles cracked through the callouses from walking what looked like hundreds of miles. She caught Helvig looking, and quickly swept her feet under her dress and out of sight.

"Your hand," Helvig said, so she wouldn't have to address the bruises around Gerda's swollen ankles. Helvig had spent plenty of long days on the road, but she had never seen someone walk themselves raw like that. Whatever Gerda was heading towards, she hadn't spared herself on the journey. It looked like she had hardly stopped to sleep.

"Oh. Yes," Gerda said. She flexed her palm and winced.

Helvig hauled herself to her feet and moved towards the other girl with her usual brusqueness, ready to take her by the wrist and examine her hand like a horse's injured hoof. But then she caught herself. If she wanted Gerda to grow to like her, she couldn't treat her like chattel. Hadn't she just given Jakko a sound beating for the same offense hours ago?

Helvig had never had any use for manners, but she got the distinct impression that if she wanted Gerda to trust her, she had better learn some.

"Let me?"

It felt strange to phrase something as a question and not a command.

Gerda extended her hand. Helvig pulled it gently to rest on her knee while she propped her foot up on the trunk beside Gerda. The witch's skin was still clammy from the biting wind, but her skin warmed under Helvig's searching touch.

"Hurt much?"

"Not terribly."

Helvig smoothed her thumb over the twined blue veins in Gerda's wrist, and the crosshatched lines in her palm some people said were the map of a person's fate. Gerda sat still for her, tame as a housecat with eyes twice as keen. Helvig could feel her watching her face, scrutinizing the tiny expressions she was trying so hard to keep hidden, but the thief didn't take her eyes away from her work.

Helvig unknotted the kerchief wrapped around Gerda's hand, revealing the thin, blood-blackened cut beneath.

"Scabbed over nicely," Helvig murmured. "And it isn't hot to the touch. I think you'll be alright."

Gerda was holding back a grin, but it came across as a smirk anyway. She found something about this whole exchange amusing, but Helvig couldn't put her finger on what.

"You think so, doctor?"

Helvig smoothed her finger over the fleshy pad of Gerda's thumb.

"That's my professional opinion, anyway."

"Well, for what my opinion is worth, I agree with you."

"You were very brave, out on the road today. I know you must have been scared, but you didn't show it."

Gerda shrugged.

"Fear services no one in times of trouble. And anger has a way of drowning it out."

A foreign emotion twisted in Helvig's gut. Guilt, she realized.

"Apologies for the bloodletting."

Gerda blew air through her lips, a gesture that delighted Helvig with its unabashed girlishness.

"I know why you did it. I've paid steeper prices for a roof over my head, and while I may still be cross you took it upon yourself to offer me your hospitality…I'm grateful for it all the same. I can't be choosy about the kind of mercies that come to me in this weather."

Helvig dropped her knee. She didn't realize she still lightly held Gerda's hand until the other girl squeezed her fingers.

Helvig pulled her hand away and whirled around. She took the rings from her fingers and the baubles from her ears, dropping them into the pockets of her vest for safe keeping, her face burning red all the while.

"It was good of you to play along when you met my father. He's a cunning man and I'm not sure he believed us, but it matters how things look to the men. Knowing other people's places keeps them in theirs."

Gerda chuckled, a throaty sound that sent a warm shiver down Helvig's spine.

"Does your father travel the world looking for the sorriest miscreants he can find?"

"The miscreants find him, mostly."

"Is that how he came into possession of you?"

Helvig turned around and regarded her guest warily. Gerda's tone was aloof as ever, but her eyes gleamed with interest in the lantern light.

"Guess we don't look much alike, do we?"

"With your dark coloring and his red hair? No."

"Would you like a drink?"

The suggestion fell from her mouth unconsidered, and she was impressed with her own boldness. Gerda seemed genuinely surprised, and Helvig counted it to her credit that she could get one over on the enigmatic girl.

"I...think I would like that, yes," Gerda said.

Helvig pulled the cork out of the old missionary's wine with her teeth and scrubbed out a shallow wooden bowl with the cuff of her blouse

Stories from her past swirled around inside her in waves that threatened to overtake her if she wasn't careful. She needed to dole out her secrets wisely. As ferociously as she wanted Gerda's trust, she knew better than to give away the moments that had made her too freely.

"I was six," Helvig began. "Starving on the streets while my parents rotted in the churchyard. Smallpox, I think, or maybe the influenza. Don't recall. But I remember how I would stand in the marketplace and mope until some charitable soul bought me a bit of bread. Or until a stupid one looked away long enough for me to palm his pocketbook."

Helvig poured the last of the wine into the bowl, filling their little tent with the fragrance of overripe plums and acidic Italian soil.

Their fingers brushed when Helvig passed Gerda the bowl, and the robber's heart flapped in her chest like a dying moth.

When Gerda took a sip and glanced through her lashes at her host, a rich red stain coloring the creases of her lips, Helvig felt like she was already drunk.

"One day," she continued, swallowing hard, "the encampment of ne'er do wells outside the city walls came into town to spend their gold, and I was stupid enough to try and lift a silver dagger right off King Berthold's hip. Course, it was too big for me to filch properly, and of course he caught me. You've seen him; I was terrified he was going to put me in a mince pie and eat me in two bites."

"What stopped him?"

"The prospect of another pair of hands working the roads, I s'pose. He said I was the lightest-fingered six-year-old he had ever seen. He swung me up on his shoulders and stuck an apple in my mouth and carried me home like a prize piglet." She recalled her terrified disbelief that anyone could want her at all, and the way she cried for joy when he had bought her a meal fit for a king at the local tavern. She could still taste suckling pig and hot buttered bread and malty brown ale, and warmth swelled in her chest at the memory. "He took me to raise, taught me proper thieving and hunting. Just like that, I was someone's daughter again. Look."

Helvig retrieved a dagger slid between the bindings of her furry boots, and she held it up to the lantern light. The flames danced along the fine etching of the blade and illuminated the glossy curve of a mahogany handle.

"This is that very knife. He gifted it to me, as a reminder."

"A reminder of what?"

Helvig gave a sly look.

"To never let my eyes get bigger than what my hands can carry."

"It's beautiful. May I admire it?"

Helvig leaned forward to hand the weapon over, but she stopped short at the last moment.

Mind what I said about trouble, her father whispered in her ear.

"Oh, I see, clever witch," Helvig drawled, withdrawing her knife. "I shall keep my weapon, thank you, out of sight and close at my side in case you try anything during the night."

"Oh, what would I possibly try?" Gerda asked with a pout. She affected innocence well, but Helvig could see by her eyes she had been thwarted. Maybe not in something so brazen as a murder plot, but definitely in some sort of machination that would weaken Helvig's tenuous upper hand.

"You're a smart girl; you would have figured something out."

Gerda merely smiled a mutineer's smile and began to hum a song used to frighten children into sleep. She unwound her braids with nimble fingers and brushed the free strands with a small comb she carried in her purse

"So," Helvig said, shucking off her heavy oilcloth jacket. She was trying not to stare at all that hair, or think of how badly she wanted to touch it. "I've told you a bit of my tale."

"So you have."

"What about you? Why are you so keen to die at the top of the world? What's waiting for you up there?"

"My business is my own," Gerda said flatly.

Helvig swallowed her frustration. They had shared food and drink and shelter, and she was doing her best to prove that she meant the girl no harm. What more could Gerda possibly need to feel safe sharing her story?

"As you've said. And this Snow Queen, she's your business too?"

"I've said as much."

Helvig made a derisive sound.

"The same Snow Queen children press hot pennies to frosted windows to see? The white lady who paints the flowers with ice?"

Gerda's eyes flashed a warning. This anger was very real, and it burned hotter than Helvig thought such a chilly creature could manage.

"That's a fairy story."

Helvig tossed her coat in a corner and began to unfasten the gaudily buckled belt around her hips. Gerda stood and lazily pulled at the laces on the back of her dress.

"So are you, witch," Helvig grumbled. "And so am I, for that matter. A little girl in Torino saw me relieving her family of some fowl one night and now there's a whole village of Finns who think there's a wild girl raised by wolves living in the woods, eating chickens, feathers and all. All fairy stories start with some terrible truth, and that's the teeth of the thing. That's the bit that sinks into people and makes it so they never forget. It's almost always the ugliest part of the tale. So, what's yours?"

Gerda's outer dress slipped from her shoulders and pooled at her feet. Helvig's breath caught in her throat at the sight of Gerda clad only in a shift, and if she didn't know better than to indulge such a fantasy, she would have thought that Gerda had done this on purpose, to distract her.

The witch stepped unabashed onto the bower of furs.

"I didn't realize the price of sharing your bed was my life's story."

Helvig shimmied out of her breeches and stood in her oversized undershirt, still clutching her father's knife. Gerda, in her supine position, posed no real threat and yet Helvig felt like she was about to slip into bed with a huldra who wanted to draw her into dark and twisting labyrinths she would never escape.

"It's a better deal than what Rasmus had in mind."

"You're still upset about that, aren't you?"

Gerda looked better than a dream, ten times more fetching than any ballerina.

Insinuations leapt to mind, too many to easily corral.

"Fine," Helvig grumbled, side-stepping this new and dangerous topic of conversation. "Take your secrets with you to your grave for all I care. Just don't drag me down with you."

She sank down next to Gerda, slipping under layers of knit

wool and soft pelts. Her knife, as always, was slid underneath her pillow.

"Do you take your knife to bed with you?" Gerda asked, blinking her huge blue eyes. "That seems rather unsafe."

"Unsafe? How am I s'posed to stay safe at night *without* a knife in my bed? You're a funny girl."

"Well, witches need not explain their ways to mortals," Gerda said with a yawn.

Helvig rolled over onto her side so that she and Gerda lay face to face. Gerda's pale hair was spread out around her on the pillow like a bridal veil.

"Shoot straight with me," the thief said quietly. Gerda's brow softened a bit, allowing whatever question may follow, and Helvig's heart beat quick in her chest. "Are you really a witch?"

Gerda considered this for a moment, fair lashes shielding her eyes.

"I know the properties of a few herbs, and I can divine weather from the clouds, and I am a woman who travels alone on the wide roads of the world. If that makes me a witch, then I suppose so. But I don't think I'm the sort of witch your boys hope I am."

"Then what's that around your neck?"

Gerda touched the charm pressed against her breastbone. Some of the ice behind her eyes began to thaw, just like when she had met Bae.

'It's a prayer, written in runes and baked into clay. Someone gave it to me a long time ago, to keep me safe on my journey."

"Is it magic?"

"In a way, I suppose. I never take it off, so maybe I believe it is."

Helvig reached out and ran a fingertip across the hard grooves of the clay. An illicit thrill went through her, both from touching such a devilish item and from feeling the warmth of Gerda's skin through her thin shift.

Helvig pulled her hand back to her side of the bed quickly,

stuffing it under the blankets. She shouldn't touch her, if she could manage it. She shouldn't even look at Gerda too closely, not after what happened last time.

"It's beautiful."

"Thank you," Gerda said, and tucked the necklace back into her shift. She pressed her fingertip into the knife under Helvig's pillow, just hard enough to dimple the skin.

"It really is lovely, this blade. You should be proud to carry it."

"I am," Helvig said, and her voice came out strangely hoarse. She snatched up the lantern from beside her bed and blew it out without ceremony, welcoming the darkness that obscured her features from Gerda's unrelenting gaze. "Well, we ought to sleep. Morning will come soon enough."

"What then? Shall I be your little pet, kept on a golden leash until you get tired of looking at me?"

Her tone was idle, softening the cutting edge of her question. If anything, she sounded weary, and Helvig wondered if she was used to being kept in fine cages and marveled at by her captors.

That twist of guilt came back again.

"Of course not. You'll have to think of some way to make yourself useful to the camp, otherwise the King will make me drop you right back where I found you. You said you were grateful for our hospitality and I'm happy to extend it, but you heard my father. We all must earn our place here."

"You need food, don't you? I'll find some."

"Are you a forager?"

"When I have to be. But I was offering to go out on the hunt for you. I'll bring your father a fine catch of venison and then he'll have nothing to complain about."

Helvig propped herself up on an elbow and glanced inquiringly over to the slight girl lying beside her. She didn't look like she could last one minute in a brawl. She certainly didn't look strong enough to wrangle wild game and drag it back to camp.

"You're joking."

"Why should I be? I'm wicked with a bow and knife." Gerda fixed her with a faux somber look. "I once felled a moose single-handedly when I was out on my own in the forest without a bite to eat."

"You didn't!" Helvig giggled, and Gerda laughed in return, her nose crinkling like paper.

"I'm not quite as good a liar as Rasmus, am I?"

"Not yet, anyway."

A strange feeling was bubbling in Helvig's chest, making her feel lightheaded. This was a pleasure she had never known; the warmth of another girl beside her in her own bed, to whisper secrets to and giggle with.

Gerda gave a contented sigh and burrowed deep into the softness of Helvig's blankets, letting her eyes slip shut. When was the last time she was able to sleep in a proper bed? Helvig couldn't keep the question from crossing her mind any more than she could stop hypothesizing about who Gerda really was, underneath the ice and the formality.

Helvig had never wondered much about her marks until now, only about how much gold they might be carrying and how long it would take them to reach the nearest town and raise an alarm. But Gerda was not a mark, and with every passing minute Helvig grew less sure that she was a powerless guest beholden to Helvig at all.

All her life Helvig had worn imperiousness like a crown, moving through the kingdom her father had created with all the assurance divine right bestowed. But now she felt like a guest in an unfamiliar court, one that spoke a strange new language of half-truths and surreptitious glances. In the court of intrigue Gerda was queen, and she could strip Helvig bare with one flick of her eyes without ever having to reveal a single one of her secrets.

I will riddle you out, Helvig mouthed to the dark, and then curled up on her own side of the bed. She fell asleep to the lull of Gerda's breath beside her, as steady and hypnotic as the sound of waves breaking against rock.

SIX

The dream descended darkly, pulling Helvig through the cold black of unconsciousness into somewhere twilight-lit and barren.

Icy wind lashed her hair and her face throbbed where it was pressed against the ground. Pain pounded through her veins with every beat of her heart, and fear soured her stomach

Someone dragged her up by the collar of her shirt until her toes were barely touching the ground, and Helvig's ribs seared with pain. A fracture, maybe, or bruising so deep it purpled the bone.

Clawlike fingers tipped with fractured glass grasped her face in a vice. She was being suffocated in a grimy tangle of hair, pressed spine-creakingly tight to the chest of another woman.

Helvig knew her by her scent, by the color of her hair.
Astrid.

Helvig thrashed, arching her neck almost to the breaking point, but there was no escaping the kiss lowered to her lips. Frigid water poured over her tongue and into her mouth, filling her throat to capacity.

Helvig convulsed, but her cries were swallowed up by the crushing pressure of the demon's mouth. Spots swam in her vision as her lungs filled with burning cold. There was no recourse, no reprieve. Unconsciousness began to set in as the creature raked fingers tenderly through Helvig's hair.

A voice rose out of the roaring wind and wound around her like a snake.

Stay with me.

Stay with me here.

Helvig flew awake with sweat drying on her skin. Breath ripped through her burning lungs in a gasp. She choked but retched up nothing.

Someone spoke her name in the dark and closed a cold hand around her wrist.

Helvig thrashed, knocking her assailant with the sharp of her elbow.

Gerda hissed out a curse in Danish and cradled her throbbing jaw.

"Helvig, be still! It's me; it's just me!"

The tent swam into focus as Helvig took in her surroundings, heart threatening to burst in her chest. She was alone here except for Gerda's slim shape beneath her blankets.

Now, she remembered. The kidnapping on the road, their dance of truth-telling and secret-keeping as they undressed for bed, the way Helvig had drifted off to sleep with Gerda's breath in her hair.

Embarrassment flooded Helvig when she realized the scene she had just made.

"Gerda," she breathed. "I'm sorry."

Gerda's small hand drifted up to touch Helvig's cheek, and it came away wet. The thief didn't even realize she was crying until she saw Gerda wipe her tears off on their bed.

Gerda held the back of her hand to Helvig's forehead.

"You're so cold! Are you falling ill?"

"No, I'm fine, it was…" Helvig shuddered. She had experienced the night terrors before, but always when she was alone. She had never had to explain them. "A night terror. I was being drowned, or frozen...both, I don't know. It felt awful. Like it was real."

Gerda made her hum of knowing.

"You've been visited by an omen. I've seen this before, with merchants choosing between their investments or couples trying to conceive. There's wisdom to be riddled out here."

The witch groped for the candles Helvig kept by her bedside, and in a few moments their tent was full of the phantom glow of firelight. Gerda looked like a ghost herself as she shifted nearer to Helvig, a half-moon shoulder peeking out from her underdress.

"I know a bit of oneirocriticism. You must tell me what you saw; I will interpret it for you."

The thought of Gerda finding out she had been kissed in her dreams, by a woman no less, made Helvig's chest tighten.

"No, really, I'm alright—"

"Did you see a great black dog? Or a smiling man with no teeth? I've seen him before myself; he's very frightening. He's a harbinger of famine, you know."

"No, none of that, I saw..." Helvig swallowed hard. She could lie, of course, and spare herself from having to recount the whole sordid tragedy of Astrid. But maybe there was a way to protect her own secrets without pushing Gerda away. A half-truth would do the job. "...a woman. Tall and terrible and cold to the touch."

Gerda became very still. Her features arranged themselves into a horrible expression, cavernously shadowed by the firelight. It was half fury and half terror, and Helvig became suddenly aware of how little she really knew about this girl she had invited into her bed, or what she was capable of.

"A woman?" Gerda hissed. "Impossibly tall, with hair like a burial shroud?"

Helvig felt cold all over.

"Yes, she—"

Gerda seized Helvig's wrist. The thief would never have guessed how strong she was. Helvig grasped blindly for her knife, but her fingers clutched only air.

Gerda pulled Helvig into the light, and just as Helvig was beginning to wonder whether she was going to have to break that pretty nose to be let go, she realized that Gerda was only examining her. With an intense, harsh scrutiny that frightened her, but only examining her.

"God's blood, Gerda, what are you *doing*?"

Gerda's eyes roved across Helvig's face and throat, and then she touched her fingers to a spot on Helvig's neck that felt tender. Helvig had not been injured when they had retired together, and the painful touch recalled her night terror moments ago. Had she clawed at herself in her sleep? Or had she somehow really been bruised by the creature that had swept her up in a dream?

Gerda sucked air through her teeth, warding off the Devil.

"It's her mark. The Snow Queen's."

Despite her disorientation and the fear still coursing through her veins, Helvig couldn't help but laugh.

"You're joking."

Gerda pulled off her charm of runes and herbs and draped it around Helvig's neck.

"You must sleep in this," she said, tucking it underneath Helvig's nightshirt so the charm rested against her skin. It was still warm from lying close to Gerda's body. "It will protect you from her if she comes back."

"Gerda, please, this is nonsense. How can *you* be sure what *I* saw in a dream?"

Gerda fixed her with a dead-eyed look.

"She kissed you and you felt as though you would die from the coldness of her, but you were powerless to escape?"

Helvig stiffened. Was she so transparent? Did she wear her crooked nature on the outside of her skin, like a poisonous flower that bloomed scarlet to keep hungry animals away?

"Yes, but how did you—?"

With a ripple of blankets, Gerda was out of bed and on her feet. She snatched up the lantern.

"Gerda!" Helvig hissed, remembering at the last moment to lower her voice. At the rate they were going they were going to wake the whole camp. "Get back into bed! This is nonsense."

Gerda paid her no heed, just pushed her way through the tent flap, swinging a wide beam of yellow light into the night outside.

Helvig lunged for her breeches and tugged them on crookedly.

"Gerda! It's pitch-black, you'll freeze!"

But she was already gone. Helvig ripped the fur pelts from her bed, scrambling around for her knife until she found it tangled up in a blanket. Snatching it up, she darted outside.

Gerda was standing barefoot in the snow, her thin shift rippling against her legs in the wind. Her hair writhed like a tangle of snakes as she shouted up into the night.

"You stay away from her! I know what you are and I'm not afraid of you! I won't let you take her!"

Helvig had never seen someone lose their grip on sanity, though Rasmus had plenty of stories about men going mad and throwing themselves in front of bullets. She was terrified she was witnessing something like that now, and she was sorely ill-equipped to deal with it.

"You'll wake the entire camp," she hissed lamely, for she could think of nothing else to say. "Foolish girl!"

Gerda spun to and fro to peer into the tops of the trees and the shadowy alleyways between tents.

"I'm coming for you!" She continued, oblivious to the lights that were coming on in the camp, or the irritated grumbles that were rising from tents a little ways off. "I'm going to find you and I'm going to get him back! I'll kill you if I have to! Do you hear me? I'll kill you!"

Helvig had do something, and quickly. Coercion and speech had failed her, so she fell back on the great standby of her life: brute force.

She threw an arm around Gerda's mouth and began to wrestle her back towards the tent like a young reindeer gone astray from the herd. Gerda shrieked against the muzzle and kicked up snow with her tiny blue-toed feet until finally, halfway back to the tent, she relented. Helvig half ushered, half shoved her inside the tent, and then peered nervously outside her door to see if anyone was coming to investigate the ruckus.

In the end, the sounds of irritated men's voices died down, and the lights around camp went back out.

"What on earth," Helvig asked, throwing the flap closed. "Was that?"

Gerda was sitting with her head in her hands on the edge of Helvig's bed. Her shift was wet around her calves, pressing transparent against the skin, and her poor feet looked well on their way to frostbite.

The last time Helvig had seen a woman so possessed by emotion, it had been when one of the little children in the camp had fallen into a cooking fire, and his mother had reached in with bare hands to pull him back out. The woman's hands had been mottled with burns for a week, but she said that she had felt nothing when she rescued her child except fear, and love. Helvig could only imagine what Gerda loved enough to make her so heedless of her own safety.

"You've been visited by the white lady," Gerda said, as though this explained everything.

Helvig pinched the bridge of her nose between two fingers.

"I had a nightmare, Gerda. There was no magical woman in a crown of ice, it wasn't like that, it was…"

Helvig was still frightened, and that made it increasingly hard for her to string her words together. They felt like tiny embroiderer's beads that were slipping through her fingers and bouncing too far away for her to reach. She wanted to set Gerda straight, to clear her mind of this ridiculous bedtime story that she was so obviously fixated on, but that would involve telling the truth. Telling the whole story about Astrid, and the wedding. And Helvig didn't think she was strong enough to do that.

"You saw the Snow Queen," Gerda insisted. Her eyes were ferocious, lit from within by fear and other darker emotions that Helvig could not name. "She who comes in the night to poison the minds of children and steal them away."

Helvig shucked off her breeches, wet and cold from their midnight excursion, and tossed the knife down on the bed beside Gerda.

"Well I'm not a child, and you said The Snow Queen was a fairy story. Is she, or isn't she?"

Gerda pressed her lips together and refused to look at Helvig.

A lick of anger flamed up in Helvig's stomach, and she didn't know what to do with it.

"Listen, you had better start answering my questions or I'll—"

"Or you'll what? Tickle me with your knife? You're going to have to do better than that."

Helvig curled and uncurled her fists a few times, a torrent of words building in her throat. She was sure the dam would break any moment and she would say strange and cruel things, things that would even surprise her.

But in the end, the dyke held fast, and the river of words slithered back down into her stomach to fester.

She took a deep breath, and then snatched up a rag from the ground. Assuming responsibility for Gerda meant watching out for her not just when she was pretty and clever, but when she was combative and frightened, too, and Helvig had made a promise to her father.

Helvig knelt in front of Gerda and pulled one of her battered feet up into her hands.

Gerda made a sound that was more bird than girl and yanked her shift back down over her feet.

"What are you doing?"

Helvig sighed heavily. The late hour was getting to her, and Gerda's newfound ability to fly from cool reason to madness without provocation was exhausting.

Helvig let her head slip down to rest against Gerda,

forehead pressed to knee, and then straightened back up and fixed Gerda with a steely gaze. It was strange, looking up at a girl who, when standing, barely came up to Helvig's shoulder. But it wasn't unpleasant.

"I won't let you bring your freezing, wet feet into my bed, and I'm worried you may have injured yourself running off into the ice like that. Sit still and it'll be over soon, and I promise it won't hurt too much."

"I…"

Gerda's voice faltered. She still wore a wild look.

"You what? You don't like people to touch you?" Helvig was being uncharitable, but it was difficult not to let frustration into her voice. "I'd have thought someone so well-off would be used to having ladies stoop to wash their feet."

"My family was never wealthy," Gerda said, and Helvig was shocked to be given one of Gerda's well-guarded personal details so thoughtlessly. Perhaps her excursion outside had rattled her, weakening her defenses. "We didn't have house servants. I just don't like people making a fuss over me when I'm hurt."

"You've chosen the wrong bedmate, then. In this camp we take care of each other, and I'm responsible for my people's health and well-being as well as their conduct. Don't shame me by refusing care when you so obviously need it." She softened her voice a bit. "There's no need to be embarrassed."

Gerda still looked frightened, but slowly, ever so slowly, she nudged her feet forward to where Helvig could reach. She tugged her shift up around her knees, exposing her knobby ankles and battered toes.

Helvig washed the cuts out with the rag and melting snow the best she could, picking out woodland debris with her fingers. It could not have been comfortable, and little jolts of worry shot through Helvig every time Gerda stiffened or hissed in pain. When Jakko got something sharp lodged in his foot, Helvig held him down and ignored his hollering while she yanked it out. But this was delicate work, and it felt more weighted.

She glanced up to scan Gerda's face, and found that the girl was staring down at her with something close to wonder in her eyes, or bafflement.

"Don't people ever do anything nice for you?" Helvig murmured, lowering her gaze. It was difficult to look straight at Gerda for very long.

"Kindness always has its price."

"Plenty of things have their price. Information, people, courts...But putting a price on kindness rather defeats the purpose, don't you think?"

Gerda's pinched mouth was wary. Helvig had been raised to cheat and swindle and save her skin every chance she got. She was intimately acquainted with the black hearts of human beings, but she would still at least taste the grog men bought her in taverns before assuming it was poison. What could have happened to make this slip of a girl so suspicious?

"You need to be gentler with yourself," Helvig said, massaging a warmth back into Gerda's toes. It looked like someone had tried to take care of Gerda's feet, perhaps treating calluses and cuts with bandages or herbs, but constant wear ensured the wounds split back open before they were ever able to fully heal. "A few days off your feet as much as you can manage would do you a world of good."

"That's not possible," Gerda said, her voice tight. "I can't stop. I can't be deterred another day."

Helvig rubbed the rag briskly up and down Gerda's shapely calves, stimulating the flow of blood.

"Sorry to hear that, but it doesn't change facts. You're staying until after the dark days, end of discussion."

Cold steel bit into Helvig's throat, and she froze.

"I don't think you've thought this through, birdie," Helvig said. To her credit, she kept her voice level and low. This wasn't the first time in her life she'd had a knife to her throat, and in her line of work it was unlikely to be the last.

Gerda tilted Helvig's chin up with the blade until they met eyes. The thief cursed herself for being stupid enough to leave her weapon lying around where anyone could grab it, but she wasn't fearing for her life yet. Gerda was desperate, and she was scared. She wasn't thinking straight, and she had already proven she didn't have the nerve to slit a throat when such things were called for.

"Let me go," the witch whispered. "Right now. Call for a horse, and food, and send me on my way."

Helvig gave her best defiant look.

"Shan't."

Gerda's lip wobbled. She was gripping the knife so tightly her fingers shook.

"Go ahead," Helvig pressed. "Cut me. I'll scream so prettily for you, and give you plenty of blood to remember me by."

Tempests swirled behind Gerda's eyes, but she didn't relent. They would be at this all night if neither one of them did anything about it, and Helvig, for one, was very much looking forward to a little peace and quiet.

Helvig lunged forward and shoved Gerda onto her back with a speed that knocked the wind out of her. In a flash, she had clambered on top of the smaller girl and was pinning her down with her knees, both hands clawing for the knife in Gerda's deathgrip.

At first Gerda thrashed and writhed, grunting like an animal trying to escape the hunter's trap. But then her body went slack beneath Helvig and her hands opened.

Helvig retrieved the knife quite easily then, and stowed it safely on her side of the bed.

"Lesson for the wise," she panted. "There's no shame in not having the stomach for murder, but if you're going to hold a dagger to someone, you had better be ready to use it."

Gerda's face had crumpled, but she didn't cry. She just lay on the bed looking wrung-out, her eyes unfocused on the ceiling.

Helvig unwound her fingers from Gerda's wrist and sat back on her haunches, studying the witch's face. Helvig had been raised to fight for her life down to the last breath , and had never seen someone give up and slip out of their body in the middle of a tussle like this. It concerned her.

Didn't Gerda realize they were only scrapping, and that Helvig would forgive her for pulling a knife as quickly as she would forgive a beloved pup for nipping at her when it got scared?

"Gerda?" She asked softly. There was no response. "Please, won't you tell me what happened to you?"

Gerda turned her face towards Helvig. She wore her mask again, mildly irritated but placidly calm.

"If it's all the same to you, I'm very tired. I would like to go to bed."

Helvig scowled. She wanted to twist Gerda's arm like when she wrestled with Rasmus to make her tell all her secrets, or to kiss her hard, white mouth so she couldn't say anything at all.

In the end, she clambered off the other girl and left her to her side of the bed in peace.

"I'll not tolerate another scene like that. If you pick a fight with me again, I'll be sure to finish it. And when that lantern goes out you are not to leave this tent, understand?"

Helvig bent down to extinguish the lantern with a terse puff. Then she threw herself back into bed beside Gerda and curled up with her back to the other girl, a bundle of rabbit pelts pressed to her chest like a child's poppet.

"It was a nightmare, you hear me? Nothing else. I'll thank you never to speak of it in front of me again, or you'll find yourself sleeping on a sled out in the cold."

Gerda said nothing, and Helvig seethed in silence with only the weight of things unsaid for company. It sat inside her like a stone, shapeless and cold.

Helvig could not place the moment where rage faded to apathy and apathy to exhaustion, but she was asleep before Gerda had any further chance to argue or explain herself.

SEVEN

Helvig woke alone, with one arm sprawled across the side of the bed where Gerda should have been. It took a few minutes for the warm delirium of sleep to clear and the events of the previous day to come flooding back into her mind. Then she was up like a shot, hair flying in wild corkscrews around her face.

The witch had fled.

Helvig dressed in a panic and yanked her hair back with a strip of castoff leather. Her father was going to murder her if Gerda had gotten into any trouble while Helvig's back was turned.

She could have robbed us blind and made off with our spoils. She could have stolen a horse. She could have—

Helvig darted out of the tent, one arm threaded through her coat sleeve, and found Gerda sitting with Rasmus by one of the fires. He was holding up his shirt, chatting away as blithe as ever as Gerda prodded at a wound festering in his bony chest.

Helvig thought she might swoon from relief, but her gratitude that Gerda was present and accounted for was quickly replaced by prickling irritation.

She yanked on her coat and stamped on through the snow.

"The bullet ricocheted right off the tree and grazed my side. Jakko didn't even notice he had shot me at first, he was so shaken up about having to shoot at anyone at all. He couldn't hit the broad side of a moose if it lay right down in front of him, I tell you."

Gerda daubed at his skin with a strip of cloth she had boiled until it steamed.

"You're very lucky you were only grazed. A few more inches to the left and you would have ruptured your spleen."

"That's bad, is it?"

"Quite bad."

"What's all this?" Helvig asked, rubbing her fingers together briskly to ward off the cold. In her haste to find Gerda she had forgotten her mittens.

Rasmus looked up at her, a smile splitting his battered face. He had always managed to keep his boyish charm and even a passing semblance of good looks, despite that unfortunate nose that hadn't been handsome even before several fists had become well-acquainted with his face.

"She's using her magic on me, Helvig! Just like in the stories!"

"Is she now?"

Helvig approached the tiny cauldron simmering over the fire, hoping for some oats and milk or maybe a bit of meat. But all she found were pungent herbs steeping down to nothing in a frothing boil. Helvig pulled a face.

"Don't tell me this is breakfast."

"It's a potion," Rasmus said. "Any idiot can see that."

"Old man's beard and devil's nettle," Gerda said. "To ward off sickness and fester."

Helvig peered down at the bullet wound on Rasmus' side. She had of course seen it when it was fresh; she had stripped Rasmus of his filthy shirt and wadded it up to staunch the bleeding while she screamed a blue streak at Jakko. The merchant they were targeting had fled without dropping a single silver piece, and Jakko had sulked for three days.

But now, the jagged tear was swollen and painted an angry

shade of red, with pustules full of yellowish infection spread across the area.

Helvig hissed through her teeth and spat over her shoulder.

"Christ on the cross, Rasmus! That looks bad. You told me it was getting better!"

"Well it was and then it wasn't. I didn't know what to do about it, so I just tried not to touch it or sleep on it."

"That'll kill you, boy."

"She's right," Gerda said. "You're lucky the infection isn't already in your blood. You would have been dead in a week."

Rasmus paled, but he soldiered on as Gerda drained his sores and wiped them clean with her cloth.

"Lucky me then, to have found such a wise and beautiful sorceress to take pity on me."

"You didn't find her Rasmus, I found her."

"As I recall," Gerda said mildly, swirling the herbs around in the cauldron with a wooden spoon. "I was the victim of an incompetent group ambush. And the last time I checked I still belonged to myself, so I'll allocate my magic as I wish."

"Of course, miss witch," Rasmus said, and winked at Helvig. "Where did you learn your craft, anyway?"

"I apprenticed with a cunning woman. She taught me how to mend bones and sew up knife wounds, how to deliver babies and cure them of colic. I assisted her with many a healing." Gerda cast a sparkling glance to Rasmus, lowering her voice to a whisper. "And many a dark rite."

Rasmus beamed as though Christmas had come early. Despite her best efforts, Helvig couldn't help but smile too. Rasmus always had an incorrigible weakness for tales of valor and sorcery, and if he wanted to go on believing that Gerda was a mistress of magic, Helvig wasn't going to stop him.

Gerda spooned out the nettles and twisted bundles of lichen onto a clean cloth and began to pat them dry.

"This poultice should take some the swelling down and relieve a bit of the discomfort. No matter what you do, don't try to change the dressing yourself or scratch at the blisters.

That will just make them spread. In the meantime, try to eat as much raw garlic as you can stand. It will help you heal."

"That's it then?" Rasmus asked. "No magic words or anything? I figured you would have to sacrifice a chicken, at least."

Gerda raised her eyebrows and glanced down at her hands. Helvig spied she was thinking something up, quick as a flash.

"Of course there are magic words. You must say the Lord's prayer three times over the injury at sunrise and sunset for nine days. Put your trust in the magic, and you will be healed."

Gerda scooped up a fingerful of hot herbs and pressed them to Rasmus' side. He yelped in pain, but pulled a brave face as she worked with nimble fingers to cover the infected area. Then Gerda wrapped a length of clean cloth tightly around Rasmus' middle, taking great care to press the layer of greenery flush against his skin.

"Where did you get those dressings?" Helvig asked. Their camp didn't have much in the way of medical supplies, and those with rudimentary skills in wound care and bone-setting tended to guard their tools jealousy.

"I asked nicely."

"Witchcraft," Rasmus said, laying a finger aside of his nose.

"Done," Gerda pronounced. "I'll try to see if I can't make you a tincture for the pain, but no promises. People around here seem very unwilling to part with their vodka."

Rasmus took up Gerda's hand and planted a hearty kiss on the back of her wrist.

"Thank you, Gerda, for showing your favor to this poor wretch. I shall say my prayers every morning and night and thank God for your witchcraft."

He hopped up and clapped Helvig on the shoulder, then bounded off to whatever dirty deeds the day had in store for him.

Helvig whistled lowly.

"Amazing. Getting the prince of rubbish and lies to say his prayers, as easy as you please. You could have told him to do anything for you and I bet he would have. Next time tell him to do my chores for me, will you?"

Gerda chuckled as she cleaned up her supplies.

"I'll see what I can do. He's not a bad lad, really."

Helvig watched him stride up to some of the men and start gabbing, probably boasting about the powerful rites he had just borne witness to.

"S'pose not. Just reckless and a big of a braggart, but who isn't around here?" She worried at her thumbnail with her teeth. "Certainly seems to have eyes for you, though."

Gerda shrugged.

"He can look all he likes; it won't kill either of us."

"No, of course not, it's just…"

Gerda's eyes flitted up with a question behind them, and Helvig's words dried up. She shifted her weight from one hip to the other, desperately hoping she looked casual.

"What did you mean last night, when you said you were immune to the charms of men?"

The same slow, pleased smile that had appeared when Helvig had been flustered and babbling about her men spread over Gerda's face. It was becoming plain how much she enjoyed getting under Helvig's skin.

"I meant just what I said. I don't fawn on boys like some girls do. As a matter of fact, no male of our species has ever managed to catch my eye, though I have seen some valiant attempts."

"Ah." Helvig worked a furrow into the ground with the toe of her boot. There was another question she wanted to ask, loitering just out of her grasp, but she couldn't bring herself to reach for it.

Gerda watched her fidget for a moment, then dipped her chin to her chest to disguise a laugh.

"Listen to me Helvig…I'm sorry for my conduct last night. Truly."

Helvig wasn't sure if she was talking about running out

into the snow or threatening her with a knife, but she was willing to accept the apology on either account.

"People do funny things when they're afraid. I won't hold it against you. And, ah..." Had she always been such a squirmer? She couldn't stay still when Gerda's eyes were on her, and now she tugged at her fingers. "I stand by what I did, not letting you leave in the middle of the night. But...I don't want you to feel like a prisoner. I would like to keep you, and I would like to not see you freeze on some roadside...but I won't force you to stay."

Gerda looked her over with those relentlessly searching eyes. Then she said,

"Good."

She rose to her feet, prim and self-assured and so very different from the half-mad creature Helvig had dragged into her bed last night. She wasn't sure she would ever understand Gerda, but she still felt compelled to try.

"Well we'd ought to get going, don't you think?" Gerda said. "Don't want to lose too much of the daylight."

"Go? Go where? You're staying?"

"For another day or two? Yes. I'm too badly injured to make another long journey right away, you were keen enough to say so last night. And we're going out on the hunt, of course. I told your father of my intentions this morning and he gave you his permission to accompany me into the forest. It seems he doesn't want you to let me out of your sight."

Helvig could hardly believe it. She bothered her father for gifts and gold as much as any other girl, but most people had the good sense not to assert their right to demand favors from him without first proving their loyalty.

"You just sauntered up to the Robber King and told him what for, did you?"

"That's right. He said you would know which horses to take."

Gerda began to walk briskly across the snowy ground to the patch of trees where the many horses that Helvig's father had stolen were tied up. A skinny youth had just finished giving them their breakfast and was combing out their coats with a wiry brush. Helvig jogged to catch up with Gerda and waved the youth on to his next task.

"How on earth did you convince him to let you take out the horses? He hardly ever lets me go riding."

"I asked nicely."

Helvig untied a sleek black mare, her favorite mount, and a stocky cream stallion for Gerda. The animals looked beautiful together, a perfect pair of opposites.

"Well no matter how nicely you ask me, don't think I'll be giving you a bow and arrow. I don't fancy the idea of getting shot in the back, sorry for saying so."

"After last night? I don't blame you."

Helvig ran her hand down her horse's glossy neck and gave him a loving thump. As much as Gerda's boldness shocked her, she was happy for it. It had been too long since she was let loose on a horse with no simpering boys to slow her down or draw her into asinine conversations. She craved the whip of wind through her hair, the racing rhythm of a powerful animal beneath her.

"Speaking of which, how do I know you aren't just going to make off with one of our horses and leave me for dead in the middle of the woods?"

"You'll be mounted too; you could chase me down. Alternatively, we could just learn to trust each other."

Helvig tried and failed to read her expression.

"Hmph. I s'pose."

Gerda let her stallion snuffle at her hand, and the same tenderness that had appeared on her face when she met Bae softened her features. She raked her fingers through his mane and cooed at him like a baby while Helvig tightened a saddle to his back.

"You certainly seem to love animals."

"I do. And I haven't ridden a horse in ages."

Helvig smirked as she swung herself up onto her mare. The cold December wind filled her nostrils with the scent of spruce, and her skin prickled with excitement at the thought of getting far away from camp with Gerda at her side.

"Good. Then you shouldn't have any problem keeping up."

EIGHT

Snow flew up in great white splashes as the horses galloped through the forest of birches and fir. The doe in front of them careened forward, tripping lightning-quick across the icy terrain. More than once, her slim dappled body almost disappeared in the rolling hills of snow, but Gerda shouted her horse on, never once losing sight of her quarry. Her hair flew behind her like wheat rippling in a field.

Helvig kept close pace, kicking her black mare on over field and fen. Svíčka winged circles overhead as they ran the deer to the point of exhaustion, their horses foaming and steaming at the mouth. The crow's eager cries pierced the clear blue of the sky.

Every sound and gust of wind made Helvig feel more than alive. Gerda's charm thumped against her chest, and she found that even though she didn't believe in witches or their charms, it made her feel a little stronger, a little safer.

The deer banked hard around a boulder in an attempt to shake off her assailants, but lost speed in the process. Helvig snatched an arrow from the quiver strapped to her back and threaded it into her bow, firing at the animal.

Her arrow shattered against the boulder. Helvig roared a curse, her arm aching from countless failed shots.

"Missed again!" Gerda cried, almost manic with glee.

"You're enjoying this far too much!" Helvig shouted back, yanking her horse on after their quarry.

Gerda threw back her head and laughed. Her ringing laughter had haunted the deer for the last few miles, and the sound had a quality that made Helvig shiver with delight. The gold around Svíčka's ankle glinted in the thin sunlight, flashing a bright slash across Gerda's face. She looked wild as a pagan goddess and bright as an icon of Mary, sanctity and sin all shining together as one.

"I thought highwaymen were supposed to be good hunters," she said.

"I'm still learning to shoot from horseback," Helvig replied, pulling her horse nearer to Gerda's. She could see the sheen of sweat on the stallion's flank. "I'd like to see you try it!"

"Fine!"

"What?"

Gerda thrust out her hand for Helvig's bow and an arrow. Helvig glared at her and pulled ahead, just in time to guide her horse into a leap over a fallen log.

She wasn't ready to give up, not yet.

Helvig skittered down an embankment towards the doe, who bleated with fright. She thought with the high ground she may be able to land a clearer shot, but she overshot by an easy three feet and the animal bounded away unharmed.

After yet another failed attempt to bring the deer down and another arrow lost to the forest, Helvig let out a groan. She should have trusted her instincts and gone out on foot in the snowshoes. It would have taken her an entire day to track down a deer and haul it home, but at least she wouldn't feel like such a failure.

"Come here," she called over to Gerda. "Here's your chance to prove you weren't lying about that moose."

Gerda rode up beside her, fire in her eyes, and Helvig gave her the meanest glare she could muster. She had to shout to be heard over the trammel of hooves and the crunch of snow underneath.

"Shoot me dead and father will send all the men out to skin you."

"If I wanted you dead, I would have smothered you in your sleep"

"Fair enough."

Helvig palmed over her bow and one of the few arrows she had left, nearly fumbling them as she stretched to bridge the gap between their mounts. Their hands touched for a moment, Gerda's slim fingers cold and real against her own. Then she was gone.

Gerda slung the bow over her shoulder and snapped the reins against the stallion's neck, pulling a few more crucial feet ahead.

The deer flew parallel to the hunting party, black hooves moving so fast they were little more than a blur.

Gerda retrieved her bow and strung her arrow, then waited until the very moment her horse crossed the deer's path to swing her arms out, draw the string back, and fire.

The doe went down hard, the arrow plunged deep into its thigh.

Helvig whooped in triumph.

The horses slowed to a cantor as they approached the wounded animal. Gerda's face was the picture of elation, and Helvig couldn't help the swell of pride in her chest. She was usually so cross when one of her men brought down an animal before she did, but now genuine delight on Gerda's behalf shone through despite her bruised ego.

Helvig's boots hit the ground unsteadily, and she swayed a bit in the transition from speeding animal to shifting snow.

"Good girl," she said, pressing her face to the mare's neck and feeling the way she panted for breath. She smoothed the mane of her horse with firm, long strokes. "You rode hard and well."

Helvig took the reins and began to lead her mare closer to the spot where the doe had fallen, carefully traversing snow drifts and branches.

Gerda was further ahead and had descended her horse in a

billow of pale skirts. The snow parted at her knees as she wound a narrow path towards the deer.

Rivulets of red were pouring from the doe's thigh. Gerda stepped lightly through the blood in her soft-soled moccasins, then bent down to slit the animal's throat faster than blinking.

Helvig loitered near her horse, and watched the light go out of the deer's eyes as Gerda gently stroked its muzzle.

The deer's gaze found Helvig's as Gerda whispered something sweet, and for one fleeting moment, girl and animal understood each other. Somehow, Helvig felt like she was the one bleeding out, slow and sure towards a death soft as sleeping.

"You should stay," Helvig said, so suddenly that the sound of her own voice surprised her. Gerda's eyes met hers across the clearing.

"Stay? With you?"

"With all of us. Until after Christmastide, at least. It's only a few weeks more." Helvig felt as though she were begging the queen herself for a stay of execution, not inviting a lost girl to share her table for a few nights more. She swallowed hard and nodded towards the deer. "I'll make you a fine pair of winter boots from her hide and hair, and then you can be on your way."

Gerda's smile was thin and knowing as the edge of a knife.

"You want to make me a present?"

"Seems only right. That doe will feed me and mine for weeks. You earned a pair of boots out of it, and I can't stand sitting around waiting for your poor toes to fall off from frostbite."

"These shoes have gotten me this far. They're fur-lined and watertight."

"Maybe in the spring, but not in this weather. Pass the holiday with us. We'll have spiced wine and good venison and listen to the boys tell their tall tales." Helvig stuffed her hands into her pockets and kicked a chuck of ice across the ground. "It isn't right, being alone on a holy day."

"I didn't realize you were so concerned with observing the

feasts and fasts."

"I'm not. But still, it isn't right. I couldn't have it on my conscience, you out there at the end of the year. Stay with us until the dark days are over, and then I'll send you on your way with new boots and a pack full of bread and ham. How does that sound?"

Gerda said nothing, just stroked the white spot between the dead deer's eyes.

"I cannot force you to stay," Helvig said.

It was too much like a plea, too much like a prayer, and Helvig felt as though she had exposed something horrible. But Gerda just sighed and rose to her feet.

"No. You're smarter than that."

Gerda thought for a long moment, squinting up at the grey of the sky. When she spoke again, her voice was soft.

"I cannot be delayed, Helvig. I am long-expected."

"By the boy at the top of the world?"

"Yes, by the boy."

Helvig clenched her hands around each other behind her back.

"Then I will send you on to him with the kiss of friendship and all my well-wishes in your back pocket. But after Christmas."

Fear crept into Gerda's eyes, a fear that made her look even more ancient, as though she were a wraith shrinking away from the sunlight come to break her curse. Then she straightened her back, and she was herself again.

"Very well. I will pass the Christmas holiday with you and your father here in the woods. I'll rest and resupply. But after that —"

"You've a queen to kill. I understand."

"Good. I'm glad we have an accord."

Helvig's heart threatened to wing right up out of her mouth. A smile of triumph split her face as Gerda turned from her to drag the carcass over to her horse.

"That we do, Miss Witch. Let me help you."

The two girls worked with silent efficiency to haul the deer onto the narrow wooden sleigh that Helvig had brought out with them. It took some straining and grunting, but in very little time they had secured the carcass and hooked the sleigh up to Helvig's stocky mare.

When they finished, Helvig beat the snow from her gloves and asked,

"You ever going to tell me?"

"Tell you what?"

"What you're running from. A girl doesn't take off into the woods in that fine a dress and shoes so ill-suited for the weather unless she left where she came from in a hurry."

Gerda's eyes leapt from tree to tree like she was keeping watch against wolves. Or worse.

"You told me your father takes in people the world no longer wants. Surely he must have taught you that sometimes the past shouldn't be spoken of."

Helvig opened her mouth to try and wheedle out more information, but she was cut off by the icy wind that came whipping through the clearing. The fierce chill pierced Helvig's clothes and snatched the breath right out of her lungs, and it made Gerda's hair snap like the tail of a kite.

"The horses!" Helvig cried, and Gerda lunged forward to seize the reins of her stallion moments before it bolted. The mare's eyes were rolling wildly in their sockets as she stamped and whinnied, straining against Helvig's grip on her bridle.

Gerda shouted something to Helvig, but the gale battering down from the north swallowed up her words. The stallion had whipped himself into a frenzy and was all but dragging Gerda across the clearing. Veins stuck out on her arms as she yanked the reins and screamed at the horse.

Another punishing blast bore down on them, but this time Helvig could make out a sound above the roar of wind and creak of bending pines. It was a sound of anguish, a horrible, sourceless wail that seemed to rise up from the very ground.

The sound vibrated through Helvig's chattering teeth, and the blood ran cold in her veins.

She knew that voice. She heard it in her sleep, every fitful night the indiscretion of her past troubled her dreams.

The voice screamed out again from the ungodly wind, and this time, it sounded awfully like her name.

"We must leave this place!" Helvig yelled, fumbling for a grip on her mare's saddle. She swung herself up onto the horse and was almost bucked down into the snow.

Gerda was faring no better, and had fallen into a snowdrift. She kicked against the icy ground and strained at the stallion's lead, but the huge animal was too strong for her. Helvig was sure if Gerda didn't let go soon, she would either get trampled underfoot or dragged to her death down a ravine.

"Leave it, Gerda! I said leave him!"

Helvig kicked her horse forward into the searing chill of the wind. The animal ran a wild serpentine path, whinnying as though pursued by the Devil himself, but Helvig managed to urge her on to where Gerda lay in the snow.

Helvig swung down and clamped her hand around Gerda's forearm, hauling her to her feet and onto the back of the mare. As soon as she felt Gerda's arms lock around her waist, Helvig wheeled the horse around and rode her as fast as the animal could manage back towards camp.

When they were finally far enough away from the phantom wind to slow to a cantor, Gerda spoke into Helvig's hair.

"What was that?"

"Christmas come early. From now on we mustn't venture so far into the forest. The veil is thinning fast."

Helvig felt a shiver go through Gerda's narrow frame.

"That voice…"

"A mirage," Helvig said, a little sharper than intended. "An illusion sent to drive us mad."

"It spoke your name."

For a moment, Helvig said nothing, just watched Svíčka as she circled overhead. The bird always looked like she was waiting for something to die, biding her time until the opportune moment.

"The fiends of this forest will employ all kinds of trickery to snare unsuspecting victims. It was just some elf mischief. A huldra maybe, or a nisse."

"Or a ghost," Gerda said.

Not another word passed between them the entire ride home.

NINE

As the days drew on, Christmas settled around the bandits like snow. Quietly but relentlessly, until they were up to their knees in it. As the nights got colder the stories told around the fires became darker, more bent towards the preternatural. The men spoke more wistfully of lovers they had lost to the arms of another or to the cruelest suitor of all, consumption. As surely as the sun sets and rises, the trickle of tradesman the bandits had been preying on dried up, and most of them settled into their tents to ride out a satiated hibernation.

Helvig knew well enough that as soon as the snow started to thaw the men would get itchy and contentious, desperate to stretch out their legs and have a go at each other like roosters in a cockfight. Then her father would spend his time sending the more argumentative of his lot out on long supply runs or quests for a few new horses to add to their stable.

Gerda, for her part, slipped into life as the Robber Princess' favorite like a new pair of shoes. There was pinching and discomfort at first, but she soon broke in her routines until they fit her snugly. She could never be accused of sloth, and was always skinning rabbits or offering to sew up the split faces of men who got into fights with one another. She seemed universally admired and was rarely denied any request. To be sure, some of this was on account of her beauty, and yet the men didn't hound her steps like wolves or salivate over the scent of her.

This amazed Helvig. Even though she was the beloved daughter of a feared criminal, Helvig had been raised in a world where women had to work doubly as hard to prove their usefulness. She had learned to fight and boast to get men to keep their hands away from her and their expectations of her toughness high. The few other women in their camp were attached at the hip to their husbands, or masters of cruelty in their own right. But Gerda simply took up the space she wanted, dragging skirts, mannered airs and all, and the men respected her. Even Rasmus, who grew cheekier as his health returned, only teased Gerda as far as she would allow him, and only in good fun. Maybe she really was a sorceress.

Helvig and Gerda passed their days in the comfortable companionship of shared chores and shared meals. The strident urgency with which Gerda had pursued her quest to the north waned, replaced by a contented assurance that her travels would resume in the future.

Despite the initial violent distrust that had sparked between the two of them, Gerda continued to share Helvig's bed, and Helvig looked forward to drifting off with Gerda's warmth nearby. Gerda often didn't sleep through the night and would start awake at any sound. On these nights, Helvig would reach over through her groggy stupor and rub a small circle into the other girl's back until she fell asleep again.

Nightmares, the thief supposed. Or memories.

The monstrous woman who had appeared to Helvig in her dreams never resurfaced, White Lady or no, and Gerda never explained her lunatic ravings their first night together. Despite her hunger to learn everything she could about Gerda, Helvig was grateful for this. She didn't want to remember that suffocating, punishing kiss, the way shame had made her cheeks burn when Gerda had questioned her about it. Helvig was happy to let the past lay down and die, and to enjoy every moment Gerda brushed against her in her sleep or huddled close against her back on the colder nights.

The boys, for their part, mostly behaved. After some time, they even began to invite Gerda to play their sleight-of-hand games with them, for which she had a ferocious natural talent. Helvig was a little cross that Gerda had won through sweetness the respect that Helvig had dragged out of all of them with threats and arm-wrestling matches, but having everyone in her charge get along was better than having them squabble.

One day, when the sunlight was thin and wan and the solstice darkness was creeping in through long shadows, she found Gerda standing on an upturned crate with Rasmus, Wilhelm, and Jakko huddled round.

Wilhelm reached up and placed a wreath of evergreen boughs on her head with his huge hands. Four stubby candles rose proud from the greenery, flickering with light. Svíčka, who was watching from a nearby tree branch, cocked her head curiously.

Jakko was appraising the scene like an artist would a painting. He rubbed the meager bristles that had just started to come in on his chin.

"Not a bad resemblance, I'd say. Though it's a pity about her dress."

Most days Gerda wore the clothes she arrived in, sleeping in her shift and borrowing a tunic and breeches from Helvig when her dress wanted for washing. Traditionally, the girl playing Saint Lucia would be robed in white, to represent her purity, and adorned with a sash of crimson to recall the blood of the martyrs.

The thick red scarf Wilhelm had knotted around Gerda's waist looked a little out of place against her cream and moss colored dress, but to Helvig, the image was perfect.

Willowy Gerda looked all the statelier for her spruce crown, and the scarf suggested a little color in her cheeks. If she had appeared to Helvig on the road dressed like this and claimed to be a divine apparition, Helvig would have believed her.

"She makes a fine Saint Lucy," Rasmus said. "Best we've had in ages. No offense, Helvig."

The Robber Princess rolled her eyes. The criminal dregs of society weren't very pious types, but the feast of Saint Lucia was almost universally observed. Even the most hardened heathen could appreciate a little light and frivolity in the dark of midwinter, and it was fun to order around whatever girl played serving Saint Lucy with her overflowing plates of food.

Being the only young girl in a camp full of men meant that when the boys started feeling festive, Helvig was usually saddled with the itching headdress of dripping wax.

But the picture was all wrong. Helvig was resolutely of the earth: steel-eyed and wild-haired and strong-armed. Saint Lucia was an ethereal creature of sanctified adoration, and Gerda fit that bill much better.

"Besides, she's supposed to be played by an innocent virgin," Rasmus continued wryly. Boys of his age loved to pass the time guessing who had been had and who hadn't. Helvig never let on either way, because it seemed like a losing game no matter what she admitted to. She had dallied with some of the other youth in the camp, and had even kissed Rasmus once when she lost a bet (he tasted like stale woodsmoke), but nothing serious had come of any of it.

And then, of course, there had been others. Liaisons outside of their close-knit community. But she wasn't sure those counted against her virginity in the way Rasmus was imagining.

Gerda smiled down at Rasmus while Wilhelm stuck a holly sprig into her crown.

"I may not be sullied by the hands of men, but I wouldn't call myself an innocent either," she said.

Her cool eyes found Helvig's, and heat flooded the thief's body from sole to crown.

"Oh, she's got secrets she's not telling," Jakko crowed, eager to join in the game.

"Been up to some wickedness under cover of night, have we?" Asked Rasmus. "Been lifting your skirts for the Devil when old Wilhelm has his back turned?"

He was only teasing her, in his crass way, but Helvig still opened her mouth to shut him up the only way she knew how; with a threat. Wilhelm saved her the trouble.

"You'll not speak so crudely to her, especially not when she's dressed as a saint!"

"I thought she was an evil enchantress come to lead the men into damnation," Rasmus shot back.

Wilhelm, to his credit, looked contrite. Once the loudest voice against Gerda joining their ranks, he had weakened in his resolve over time. Especially once he found out she liked listening to his stories.

"Witch or no, she has enough sanctity in her to respect the saint's day, and so should you. Anything else is blasphemy."

"Blasphemy is my middle name," Rasmus said with a roll of his eyes. "What's so special about the day, anyway? Somebody jog my unchurched memory."

Helvig had spent more time in taverns than in churches in her life, and she still knew the reason for Saint Lucia's day. Most children in the region did. But one of Wilhelm's hagiographies was a welcome escape from all this talk of wickedness and virginity, so she grabbed at it.

"Yes, Wilhelm, tell us the story."

"Again?"

"I've forgotten. And Rasmus doesn't know."

"Well, in that case..."

Wilhelm cleared his throat. When he spoke again, it was in the lulling baritone he used when he read to them from his Bible on the Lord's day, or told them one of his bloody Bavarian fairy stories.

"Lucia was a Christian girl who lived during the reign of emperor Diocletian, when his great persecution of the faithful made the streets of Rome run red with martyr's blood. She brought food and water to Christians hiding in the catacombs beneath the city and wore a wreath just like this one to light her way. When she refused the hand of a wealthy pagan man, having pledged her virginity to Christ alone, he reported her to the emperor. Cruel Diocletian put her through many torments, but she never wavered in her faith. When they tried to burn her alive, she continued to preach as the flames rose around her. And when they gouged her eyes out, her sight was miraculously restored. She did not give up her life until she had received her last rites from a priest, and only then could the body be laid to rest."

Jakko smacked his lips as though he had tasted something foul.

"Why are saint's lives always so grisly?"

"Everything good in this life takes bleeding for," Gerda said. "Everything beautiful is born of darkness, and of struggle, and the fertile soil of death."

Wilhelm raised his eyebrows at her. "Who taught you an idea so lofty? A man of the cloth, no doubt."

"No," Gerda said, taking his hand as he helped her step down onto the earth. Her crown of evergreen boughs blazed with light. "She was a witch."

In the days leading up to Christ's mass, Gerda continued to bless the camp with her presence, drifting from day to day like a will-o-the-wisp and disappearing as soon as anyone pressed her for details about her family or the city from which she hailed. Helvig would make up stories about her to pass the time as she helped her father count out silver pieces.

She was a princess, just like Helvig, but of a small war-torn country where it was no longer safe for her to live in the public eye. She was a disgraced society lady who had been turned out of her father's home after an affair with someone of low standing. Or maybe she really was a witch, one of the last living daughters of a dark line that had been all but obliterated by the hunts decades prior.

In every tale the thief told herself, Gerda was running, because that's all Helvig was sure of. There was a skittishness in her eyes that Helvig recognized. She had seen it in the eyes of every poor cretin that came crawling to her father after killing someone they shouldn't have talked back to, or stealing something they should never even have looked at. The dead person could have been an innocent or a scoundrel, and the quarry could have been crown jewels or another man's wife, but the story always ended the same. With legs pumping and lungs burning and a town they could never return to shrinking in the distance behind them.

Gerda's previous life remained in shadow until Christmas Eve, when she and Helvig sat hip-to-hip on a fallen pine tree, warming themselves by Wilhelm's fire.

Helvig had presented Gerda with her new boots earlier that day, in a private moment when they were dressing back-to-back in Helvig's tent. Despite her lack of modesty in every other area of her life, Helvig had insisted on this procedure, because the thought of Gerda's naked body was enough to make her feel panicked and overheated. She wasn't sure how she would handle all that hair and bare skin if it was presented before her.

When Gerda had turned around, still lacing her dress, Helvig felt more like she was handing over her still-beating heart than holding out a pair of reindeer boots. But Gerda had given her a wide smile and put them on right away.

Now, Gerda sat with her boots tucked up under her skirt, her tattered moccasins discarded and forgotten.

The boys were in good spirits, having rummaged up spiced wine and dried figs to go with their usual veal and hardtack. Helvig suspected that Wilhelm had been hoarding them since the summer months, waiting for some celebratory moment. As much as she teased him about his useless piety, she was always happy to be included in his small celebrations. Rasmus was happy so long as his belly was full, and even Jakko had been conducting himself with something close to manners at their meager Christmas meal.

Their roaring fire was perfumed with pine and cedar, and Wilhelm was telling one of his chilling morality tales, for once appropriate to the occasion.

"...So, the demons crafted an awful mirror, a mirror which showed the world as barren and ugly, and the people within it as twisted and vile. They flew from town to town laughing at the horrible images that showed in the mirror, and frightening townspeople with their own reflections. But these crafty imps became arrogant of their own power, and they flew higher and higher into the sky, hoping to frighten the very angels in heaven! God in his might struck them down for their hubris. The higher they flew, the colder it became, until the mirror became slick with dew and ice. And then, right as they reached the gates of heaven, it slipped from their claws and tumbled down to earth, and shattered into a hundred pieces. The pieces were so small they were caught up by the wind and they blew through the whole world, sticking in people's eyes and hearts."

Gerda gave a little shudder of delight. She had a taste for Wilhelm's grim parables.

"How terrible."

"More terrible still is what the shards did to them. The unlucky ones who got a piece lodged in their eye see the whole world as an awful, wicked, ugly place. They cannot even see the beauty in a rose, or a cathedral, or a child's smile. But it's worse for the ones struck in the heart. This miserable lot sees themselves as just as vile as the world around them, and they cannot let any love into their hearts for anything or anyone. The more they disdain themselves, the uglier the world around them becomes, and on and on and so it goes forever."

"How do you break the curse?" Helvig asked. Her eyes kept flickering over to Gerda.

Wilhelm had to think about this for a moment, stroking his short beard. He had always had a touch of the philosopher about him, and Helvig thought that if he had been given more opportunities in his youth, he may have made a fine scholastic monk, or a professor of the law.

"The only antidote would be to see oneself rightly,

perhaps. As beloved. As beautiful in the eye of another who beholds."

"Thank goodness," Jakko said, gnawing on a piece of deer jerky. "I thought you were going to say the only cure was confession and a decade of hail Marys."

Wilhelm scoffed at him, but it was good-natured. Where he got his patience from, Helvig never knew.

"It would take more than that to scrub your grimy soul clean."

Jakko gave him a greasy smile.

"Awful kind of you to say, Wilhelm." He wiped his hands on his breeches and turned his attention to Gerda. "Come on Miss Witch, it's your turn. Give us a story to feed the Yule fire with."

Gerda's eyebrows rose.

"Which one? I've got more stories than there are days to tell them in. Stories of how I knit men back together after boars gored them on the hunt, or how I cropped my hair and apprenticed as a blacksmith's boy in Halsingborg. Or how I spent a summer warming a princess' bed."

"You're making those up," Jakko scoffed, at the same moment Rasmus perked up and exclaimed,

"That one, I choose that one!"

Typical Rasmus. The slightest whisper of impropriety and you had his undivided attention. Helvig rolled her eyes, but Gerda only laughed.

"Well…she was a minor princess, and I left once the leaves started to turn, but she was dear as life to me. You really don't want to hear this silly story, though, do you?"

She addressed them all, but her eyes were fixed on Helvig. The thief took a sip of her mulled wine, never breaking eye contact, and nodded.

"Why not? It sounds like something new, for a change. And I'll never refuse a bit of your past," she added, softly.

"Was the princess beautiful?" Rasmus piped up. "Dark hair or fair?"

"Very beautiful. And she had hair as fiery as autumn

leaves."

Helvig's hand drifted up to tug at one of the small braids she wore threaded through her tangle of curls. She had never considered the color of her hair too seriously, but now it seemed a rather dull shade of unremarkable brown.

"Go on, then," Jakko said impatiently. He looked very dubious about this whole topic of conversation, and was whittling a piece of wood to a toothy point.

"I had been traveling through her city, looking for gainful employment that would replenish my purse, and I heard that the princess had a bleeding sickness that no doctor had been able to cure. Physicians had prescribed bedrest, but still she suffered. I had seen her kind of sickness before, among young women who came to the witch for help with their monthly cycles. I knew that the pain was excruciating, but that herbs and exercises could help. So, I offered up my services."

"You just walked up to a fine lady's home and asked her to hire you?" Jakko scoffed.

"Well, I said I would only collect payment if I was able to help her. That got me through the front door."

Helvig stared at Gerda. At first, she thought the witch had been joking, just spinning a bawdy tale for the fire that would rile up the boys. But there was no deception here, only the simple relegation of facts.

Helvig was as delighted to finally see Gerda open up as she was furious that she was blossoming like this in front of Rasmus and the rest, and not in private for Helvig alone.

"I sat at her bedside for days, nursing her through the worst of the pain, and I told her stories of my travels to cheer her. She was so taken by me that when she recovered, she invited me to stay with her as one of her handmaids. She dressed me in finery, taught me courtly embroidery and house husbandry and how curtsy like a lady. I loved her."

The word went through Helvig like a knife.

Love.

So Gerda was capable of it, underneath all that placidity.

And someone else had tasted her heart first.

Don't be stupid, Helvig chided herself. *You have your own history. How unkind would you be to hold hers against her?*

"But not all things are made to last," Gerda said breezily. "She became betrothed that autumn, to a kind man who could give her children and elevate her status, and we knew we had come to a parting of the ways. But she gave me Svíčka before I left, the cleverest of her tame birds. She wanted me to able to carry a piece of her with me."

"Yes," Rasmus said, leaning forward on one knee. "But what's this about bedwarming? Get to the good part."

"Some women prefer to keep their own company," Gerda said, a playful sparkle in her eyes. "And I kept hers well, soldier, I assure you."

Helvig could not believe how freely she said such things, how little shame she seemed to feel about her own proclivities. Jealousy sprawled in her chest, not just for Gerda's old bedmate, but for the way Gerda seemed so comfortable inside of her own skin.

Rasmus clutched his heart through his shirt as though struck by lightning. One of his favorite overblown gestures.

"God in heaven, girl! You're torturing me, some details please! Just…paint the picture for us a little."

Helvig wanted to die, and Wilhelm, who shirked anything remotely salacious, looked like he had one foot in the grave already.

Jakko, too shameless for propriety and too young yet to be titillated by its absence, just looked bored.

"What do I care about what girls do together? This is a stupid story. Don't you have a better one, Gerda? One without princesses in it?"

There was an earnestness in his voice that Helvig didn't often hear, and when she looked over and saw the way his eyes shined clear in the firelight, she finally saw in him what Gerda had all along. An overgrown child, scab-palmed and tough-talking. Alone in the world and all the more vulnerable for the cruelty life had taught him.

"And what kind of story would you like?" Gerda asked indulgently. Rasmus had the look of a man who had just been seated at a royal feast before being promptly escorted off the premises without a single bite passing his lips. That soothed Helvig's vindictive streak and made her feel a little better about the whole thing.

Jakko shrugged.

"It's Christ's mass isn't it? The night the dead walk abroad, and trolls play tricks on mortal families? Let's have a ghost story then, something properly frightening."

"I know the one about the ghost dogs who guard Akershus Fortress," Wilhelm proposed, looking eager to steer conversation into more orthodox waters.

Jakko pulled a face.

"That one's for babies! Come on, think of something better. What about the story of that girl in the south who disappeared? The one with the storm in it? That's a blood-chiller."

The atmosphere shifted. Something heavy settled over Helvig's shoulders, icy despite the crackling fire, and every muscle in her body tensed.

Rasmus' eyes slid over to her, wary in the firelight, and he ran his tongue across his parched lips.

"Come on, Jakko, that one's no good," Rasmus said.

"Is too! And I haven't heard it in ages. Do you have a better idea?"

"Well, I…"

He tried to catch Helvig's eye, but she was doing a very good job avoiding his gaze, or anyone's for that matter. She just stared into the fire, willing the moment to pass her by.

"I think Helvig knows it better than I," Rasmus finished. "It's hers to tell, if she wants to."

That last bit was said softly, and Helvig would have appreciated his decency if she wasn't feeling so trapped. Gerda's blue eyes glided over her curiously, and Jakko gave her an impatient look.

"Go on then, Helvig," he said. "Do your best to spook

us."

Gerda settled into her seat, folding her hands primly. She was giving over her undivided attention.

Helvig put away the last draught of her wine and cleared her throat.

"Well. There's not much to tell, it's just a townie legend. There was a girl who lived in a small village outside of Stockholm. It was before you came to live with us, Jakko. Rasmus had only just arrived and we were, what? Fifteen?"

"Thereabouts, yes."

"We were camped near the city that summer, my father and me and some of the men. We had managed to stay out of too much trouble with the authorities and some of the local children would sneak out of town to come play with me and visit Bae. It was a good season. Full of cherries and apples and laughter."

She remembered the way ripe fruit had tasted on her fingers, and on the cheeks of her playmates. It had been a heady, wild summer. The rivers themselves had seemed to bubble over with possibility and promise. Helvig had never paid much attention to her body before then but as the leaves on the trees unfurled in green brilliance, she had begun to notice the swell of new hips and breasts beneath her leathers. She had gotten her first taste of the warm excitement that overtook her when a handsome shepherd or pretty girl at the flower stall smiled at her, and she felt sure that the world was ready to open up for her and pour out delights unimaginable.

She had met Astrid that summer, when the girl's cheeks still glowed with sunlight and her honey-colored hair sat up around her ears in a braided crown. Astrid worked on the corner by the butcher's shop, selling tinderboxes and shoehorns and other small household items from her parents' shop. Helvig delighted in flashing open her little purse to show Astrid the gold she had hidden away inside.

She had stolen a silver filigree ring for Astrid, and a wooden pan pipe, and all manner of hot sugared honey hearts and cardamom buns. Sometimes, when her father wasn't paying very close attention, Helvig would sneak into the city and steal in through her companion's bedroom window by night. She could still feel the warmth of Astrid settling beside her, the hot touch of skin sticky from the summer air, the nervous brush of their lips against one another.

"There was a girl in the town, by all accounts clever and kind. She was young, in the first flush of her womanhood." Helvig stabbed at the fire with a stick. "But then her parents caught her carrying on with someone from out of town, a criminal. And so, to save her soul and their own reputation, they married her off to a man twelve years her senior, a butcher with a mewling infant his first wife had died giving birth to."

Jakko scrubbed at his runny nose.

"Is this another romance? You said it was a scary one."

"Shut up and let the lady finish," Rasmus snapped. It may have been the only time in Helvig's memory that Rasmus had afforded her the honors due her sex, and while that would have generally irritated her, now she was grateful. It somehow dignified her pain. After all, he had heard this story before. He had been there when everything had fallen to pieces, and he knew better than anyone how it had torn her apart.

"She was married on All Hallows night, a proper church marriage in front of a priest, and she immediately assumed her wifely duties in his household. By day she cooked his meals and soothed his crying child, and by night she lay down for him in the way women do for men." Helvig's stabbing of the fire increased in intensity, but she kept going. "That December, there was a storm. No, not a storm. A...terror. A wall of wind and ice that swallowed up the town. No one could leave their homes for days, and the elders said it was an ill omen of old magic, the wrath of gods long thought dead. When it was finally over, the girl's family trekked through snow up to their hips to get to her husband's house. What they found inside was terrible. Everything inside was covered in ice, from the chairs to the walls to the herbs hanging above the stove. They say that even the flames in the fireplace froze solid, but I think that's a bit of tale-stretching. But what's certain is that they found the husband's corpse on the floor, and beyond that in the couple's bedroom, the child frozen to death in her cradle."

"And the girl?" Jakko asked, eyes gleaming. This was the sort of Christmas story he had been angling for.

"Gone," Helvig said. Her voice was rough. "Fled or dead. No one knows."

"They say she called down the storm with her misery," Rasmus said cautiously. Helvig wished he would stop looking at her like she would shatter if spoken to harshly, but she was grateful that he was willing to take over the telling. She didn't have any more stories left in her tonight. "That so great was her suffering as the wife of a man she didn't love, the air and earth took pity on her."

A flicker of recognition danced in Wilhelm's eyes. "The Rus' have a tale like that, about the spirit of winter taking pity on a poor girl. They call him Morozko. They say he rewarded a suffering girl's courtesy with jewels and a marriage proposal, and punished her wicked, rude sisters with icy death."

"All fairy stories start with some terrible truth," Gerda said smoothly. She was watching Helvig so intently the thief could feel herself warming under her gaze, as though the other girl's eyes were glass magnifying a sunbeam. "Maybe the spirits of the land enjoy playing judge and jury among humans every once and a while. We must seem as children to them. So young and foolish."

"Macabre," Jakko said.

"What is?" A voice intoned behind Helvig. A meaty hand settled over her shoulder and she knew the king had decided to pay their fireside circle a visit.

"Evening Your Majesty," Wilhelm said with a tip of his head. There really wasn't need for such formal address among the dregs of their camp, but he had always been one for hierarchy. "Helvig was telling us the story of the ice storm, about that girl who went missing."

"Ah, yes," her father said. Pensiveness sounded like distant thunder in his voice. "Astrid."

Something broke inside Helvig for the thousandth time. Something that, try as she might, she had never been able to mend.

"Kind of you to join us, papa," she said with a weariness she was too tired to hide. "We were just telling some old ghost stories."

"A fine custom to keep on this bitterly cold night."

King Berthold settled his bulk down on the tree trunk beside her. He wore an extra coat of mink over his heavy oilskin and knitwear clothes as a ward against the night air. Gerda scooted over a bit to make room for him, and he spied her shoes.

"Those are some sturdy boots, little sorceress. Did my daughter gift you those?"

It was a rhetorical question, of course. He had seen Helvig hard at work scraping the fat and gristle from the deer hide and carefully stitching skin and fur together in her free hours.

"She did," Gerda said with a fond smile in Helvig's direction. "They're the warmest I've ever had."

Helvig blushed furiously and pulled her hood up around her ears to hide it.

Berthold patted Gerda's knee as though she were his own daughter, his voice kindly and warm. He was a terrifying man, by all accounts, but Helvig knew better than most that there was a soft spot in his heart for lost things. Especially children.

"And what story will you bring us on this night? I'm sure Wilhelm has already talked your ear off about the Christ child and the star and the three magicians from the Orient. I think we're overdue for something new."

"What sort of story would you like?"

Berthold leaned back in his seat and pulled out his pipe. He took his time packing the bowl with sweet spiced tobacco and then lit it with a stick and the flames of the fire. After he puffed some life into his pipe, he nodded to the tiny girl.

"I think we're all clamoring to hear how you came to be with us, and who your people were before then. Lord knows we've been patient until now."

Helvig glanced sidelong at her father past the beaver fur round her hood. *Sly old dog*, she thought. Of course he would take advantage of the traditions of the season to get Gerda to talk. None of them had been able to learn what had driven her this far north in search of a queen who didn't exist outside of nursery rhymes. They had tried, and sometimes Gerda would appease them with a snippet about her time as a witch's apprentice, but otherwise, she guarded her secrets carefully.

Gerda's smile shrank by an inch, but she did not argue. Her eyes took on that haunted, faraway look as she settled in to tell her story, resigned to her fate.

"When I was a girl I lived with my father and my mother and my brother Kai in Copenhagen. We had our rooms in a townhouse overlooking a canal, with roses in the window boxes, and my father ran a piano school for children out of the ground level. My mother was a cultured woman of letters and began teaching Kai and I to read before we could even talk. Kai is the younger. He's fifteen and I'm…" Her voice became hushed as she touched her fingers to her mouth. "Oh God. How old am I? Seventeen. I must be."

"You're the same age as Rasmus," Helvig said, hoping a bit of casual conversation would ease the telling of what was obviously a painful story. It was so unlike the somber girl to divulge her past that Helvig was afraid that if she were to speak wrongly, she would break whatever spell Gerda was under. "And he's just a little younger than me. I'm eighteen when the frost thaws."

"Kai would be a young man now," Gerda continued, absent and wan. "He was always the most responsible of the two of us. He was the boy, you see, and stood to inherit the business from my father. Kai would see to his lessons, finish his chores, and then work into the night with my father in the shop, tuning and repairing the instruments. I never had to worry about things like that. I was always weeping over cut flowers or reading silly fairy stories. Quite given to flights of fancy."

If Helvig hadn't seen Gerda glowing with delight in the presence of the animals, it would have been difficult to believe such a stoic girl was ever so frivolous.

"Kai was forced to grow up very quickly. He didn't have as much time to play as the other children, and he always knew what was expected of him. I was the only person he could be himself around. So, when he told me of a beautiful White Lady who visited him by night, I knew he was trusting me."

Helvig leaned forward with her elbows on her knees. "What did you say?"

Gerda's eyes flashed like mirrors in the firelight. "You've seen her too. She appears to those she wishes to claim. She's a dead thing, a wraith who steals children and whisks them away to die of cold at the top of the world."

"If that's the case, then why hasn't she stolen Helvig?" Jakko asked. His mouth had a funny set to it, like he couldn't decide whether to laugh at her story or shiver with fright.

"From what I can tell our princess is afraid of her, and the Snow Queen relies on her charms to entice people out of their warm beds and into her arms. Like my poor, sweet brother."

"Go on," Helvig urged. She was so tired of secrets, and she feared that if Gerda got too distracted, she would retreat back into herself and never bring up her brother again.

"As Kai grew, he became colder to me. He didn't tell me any more stories or play with me in our nursery. He only wanted to skulk about reading books or throwing snowballs at cats with the neighbor boys. He never smiled, never told me he loved me. My mother said that it was just what happened to boys when they reached a certain age, but I knew better. The Snow Queen was draining him of his life, freezing the blood in his veins with her kiss."

The king made a sound in his throat that seemed to say *of course, of course*. He was a fiend at the gambling tables and an expert at negotiating with everyone from mercenaries to washerwomen to town constables. When he got like this even Helvig didn't know what he was thinking, or if he believed a word Gerda was saying.

"One day, Kai took his little sled out into the town square. Some of the older boys were making a game of tying their sleds to the back of carriages and riding them around town, and he wanted to join them. I didn't see what happened next; I was with my mother in the kitchen, but I heard about it from the miller's boy, who came by to give his condolences later that day. A huge white sleigh no one had seen before slid into the town square, driven by a woman dressed in the latest fashions, head to toe in white. Her hair was pale as silver, and her skin had the pallor of death, and she didn't smile at any of them, only at Kai. He got it in his head to hitch himself to her sleigh, and as soon as it was done, she set off through the town with him, faster and faster, until they were through the gates and into the woods." She pressed her lips together to hold back tears. "None of us ever saw him again."

Silence fell over them all as the fire crackled. Helvig's heart felt swollen too large for her chest. She had heard many wrenching tales in her day, and every man in her father's camp carried around shameful secrets, but Gerda's story moved her viscerally. If there was any way to soothe that suffering, Helvig would happily dedicate her waking hours to it.

Eventually, Rasmus spoke.

"Why? Why take a little boy?"

"The dead despise their own loneliness, I suppose," Gerda murmured. "My mother wept for days and my father hardly spoke. They thought he had gotten lost in the woods or fallen into the canal that ran behind our house and drowned, since he had always wandered too close to it. But I knew better. I knew she had finally come for him. And I knew I had to get him back."

Her tale finished, Gerda let out a shaky breath. She let her eyes fall into her lap, and the small crew gathered around the fire exchanged fleeting, furtive looks, questioning the reality of what she had said. Except Helvig. She couldn't take her eyes off Gerda.

"You set out on foot all alone?" Helvig asked. She had assumed that Gerda had many unhappy tales to tell, and that she had been travelling for some time, but she couldn't imagine her alone for so long, with no one to squeeze her hand when she lost hope or drape her shoulders in warm blankets in the brutally cold months. "When you were just a child? How did you...?"

"Survive? Unwillingness to die. I had a child's faith when I set out that all would be well. I packed what I could, slipped out before my parents woke, and crossed the Øresund on foot. It had frozen over that year."

"I remember," Rasmus said. "But the sound between Denmark and Sweden would have been crawling with Swedish guards! We were taught to shoot any rebel we saw crawling across the ice, no matter their excuse."

Gerda shrugged.

"I was small. I got lucky. I asked around for Kai in the first town I came to and took work in a tanner's shop when I ran out of money and food. That's how I travelled, following stories of the Snow Queen north, stopping for a few months at a time in towns to work and resupply. I passed myself off as a boy until I wasn't able anymore, and then I took up women's work, sewing and midwifery and handicraft."

"That's how you seem to know a bit of every trade," the Robber King said, nodding in appreciation. Of course he had been watching her, noting her many useful skills. Nothing in the camp escaped his notice, especially when he could leverage it to his advantage.

"And when did you meet the witch?" Jakko prompted, chewing a hunk of venison.

"That was later."

"After the princess?" Helvig asked quietly. Gerda's eyes

skimmed her face and then flittered off into her own private thoughts.

"Before. I'd rather not discuss it, thank you."

An awkward silence fell, broken only by the snap and pop of burning tinder. The Robber King puffed thoughtfully on his pipe, enveloping Helvig in a thin cloud of fragrant smoke. It smelled like home, and surety, and a firm hand on her shoulders guiding her in the right direction.

After some time had passed, Berthold leaned in Gerda's direction and layed his finger aside of his nose.

"I very much hope you find your brother, birdie. Take it from an old man. Lost things tend to turn up the moment you stop searching for them."

Gerda smiled weakly. The Robber King patted her cheek and then his daughter's, rising with a groan and stretching out his aching back. He was getting older, though Helvig didn't like to think about it. He had trouble with his back on particularly cold days, and his joints creaked whenever rain was near.

"I'll leave the revelry to the young. But we're in the dark days now, so mind you watch for spirits walking abroad. The dead are fleeter of foot than you would imagine."

Jakko snorted. A boy of his age was predispositioned to turn his nose up at warnings about the things that ran wild in the unclaimed days between Christ's mass and Epiphany. He was the type to try something stupid to show his bravery, but luckily there were no nearby grave sites to disturb, so Helvig supposed he wouldn't be tempted.

"Let them try us," Jakko crowed, and brandished his stubby knife. "I'll give them a Christmas present they're not likely to forget."

Wilhelm rolled his eyes skyward, invoking some saint under his breath. Helvig could imagine him with his own children then, with that little boy who had been taken from him in the fires. He must have made a fine father, she realized, and the thought sent a pang of sadness through her. It was a night for it, she supposed. Or maybe she was becoming weaker, softer. Gerda's presence seemed to have that queer effect. Helvig thought twice before shouting at the boys now, and she forced herself to say things like please, and thank you, and I'm sorry for boxing your ears when you took the last bit of bread.

"The dead are entitled to their masses same as you and me," Wilhelm said. "Let them have the few days of the year God has allotted to them."

Gerda was standing, brushing snow off the hem of her dress. Helvig rose with her instinctively. She wanted to stoop to clear the ice from Gerda's skirts, to lift them delicately to dry them in the warmth of the fire. But such behavior wouldn't be seemly, so she tangled her fingers together and held them behind her back.

"Thank you for your stories and your companionship," Gerda said, as inscrutable and formal as ever. "Happy Christmas."

The boys murmured their goodnights, then devolved back into their own conversations just as soon as she had turned to go. None of them seemed quite as interested in Gerda's story as Helvig was, though Rasmus still had a look of sober amazement on his face. Perhaps they assumed she was lying, or had already guessed parts of her tale that Helvig had been too foolish to riddle out.

"Helvig," her father said as she turned to follow Gerda. She spared him half a glance. "Help an old man back to his bed. My back is barking."

He followed her out into the snow, leaning heavily on the arm she offered. She had harangued him about getting a walking stick, but he insisted it would make him look past his prime and invite mutiny from the muscled young upstarts who liked to cause trouble in his camp.

When they were out of earshot of the boys, he straightened a bit, not needing his daughter's assistance so much after all.

"What is it?" Helvig asked, well-acquainted with her father's tricks. This was one of his favorites to secure a private conversation.

Berthold kept his huge hand on his daughter's arm, as though she were the one who needed assistance navigating the route home.

"Quite a tale from your little friend," he said.

Helvig bristled. She didn't like the idea of her father requesting a private audience to discuss Gerda, no matter what he had to say about her. Up until this point, Berthold had given the girls a wide berth, and hadn't complained when Helvig disappeared from her usual spot sitting at his feet to spend more time with Gerda. She had sorely hoped he wouldn't bring this change of behavior up in conversation.

"We've all got our tales of woe. Hers is no different," she responded.

They were ambling not towards the king's tent but towards Helvig's, with Berthold setting their agonizingly slow pace. Already Helvig wished it was Gerda on her arm and not her father, so she could draw the other girl close and give her all manner of sweet condolences. She would be upset after telling her story. She would need comfort. A bit of bawdy gossip to make her laugh, perhaps, or a stiff drink, or Helvig holding her comb and hairpins while she brushed out her hair.

"No, I think it's quite different. I think it's told us all we need to know about your witch."

"What do you mean?"

When the King looked at his daughter, his eyes were soft with sadness. She knew that whatever he had to tell her was going to break her heart into more pieces than Wilhelm's demon mirror, and she braced for the impact.

"That girl's brother died when she was just a child, Helvig. It's a terrible thing, and a hard one, and I fear..." He took a deep breath, squinting up at the pinpricks of light in the night sky. "I fear it's driven her mad. You heard her, raving on about snow bees and fairy queens."

Helvig's skin hardened into armor.

"She isn't mad. She's a wonderful, clever girl, and she's

saner than any of us."

Berthold's voice became even more gentle.

"She could have killed that boy for all we know, and the horror of the thing snapped her mind in half. I've seen it happen, little vixen, to men stronger than her."

Helvig recoiled from her father. Not even her childhood nickname could soften the cutting edge of his words.

"That's a terrible thing to say!"

"I don't say it to be unkind, merely cautious."

Helvig ground her teeth together.

"I won't abandon her," she said, voice thick with tears. Helvig hardly ever cried, and detested people seeing it when she did, but her father disapproving of Gerda was too terrible to bear. It meant he could send her away and forbid Helvig to speak to her again. "She isn't hurting anyone and she's still my guest, and my friend. I must take care of her. I *want* to, papa."

"I've known that from the start. There's no shame in the affection that sometimes passes between girls. I don't fault it against your character, and Gerda has made a fine companion for you, for a time. But you must see reason."

Helvig's face burned. They'd had this discussion before, and she hoped to avoid it the second time around. It hadn't saved anyone then, and this affection Berthold spoke of had gobbled up everything good that she touched and nearly burned down a town, but still her father refused to blame her. That was well enough, she supposed, but she would carry the guilt of Astrid with her to the grave.

Helvig was different now, stronger, more guarded. She could handle the way Gerda mixed her up inside, at least for a little while longer, and no one had to die for it.

"Whatever you may think about any…impropriety. It isn't true. We haven't…I've been a perfect host."

They had reached Helvig's tent. Inside, the thief knew, her companion waited for her in bed, probably already undressed and drowsy-eyed.

Berthold took his daughter's shoulders in his hands,

looking into her face. His eyes had the gentle cast he reserved solely for her, his most precious piece of stolen treasure.

"Do you not think I can see into the heart of my only daughter?"

Helvig's lip wobbled. The king gave her space to speak, but she said nothing, just pressed her lips together until they lost all feeling. She would not cry. Not over this. It would be admitting too much, and even though her father could see into her like glass, she still had her pride.

Berthold sighed, releasing his daughter. He knew when not to push.

"This is your business, Helvig. But don't let it get out of control. The boys need you, the camp needs you. I don't want to see you wrecked again. Remember Astrid."

Helvig felt as though a ghost had passed through her. A wave of cold with no shape and no purpose. Just numbness and death.

"I remember."

The Robber King kissed his daughter's head and she stood still for him, silent tears rolling down her cheeks. Then he turned and trekked off through the snow.

When he was gone, she took a gasping breath. Helvig smudged her tears off her face with the edge of her sleeve. Gerda would be missing her. She needed to get inside.

She found the witch sitting on the bed, brushing out her impossibly long hair and singing softly. She had stripped down to her shift but was still wearing her furry reindeer boots.

"What did your father want with you?" She asked lightly. Too lightly, Helvig thought. Maybe she already suspected that Berthold had not taken her entirely at her word.

"Nothing interesting," Helvig replied in a hollow voice. Try as she may, she had never been able to hide her feelings like Gerda could. Every impulse and injury burned right out of the lantern of her body for all the world to see. "Business chatter."

"Business? Something wicked, I hope." Gerda's coy,

prying smile curled through Helvig's stomach in a tingle of heat. "Plotting another kidnapping?"

Helvig's smile was tight. God, she was weary, and she didn't know how to look at Gerda without getting hurt in the process, but she must try to be friendly and sisterly. Especially tonight, after she had shared such an awful story.

"No, you were a one-off."

No sooner had she thought of Kai than she was reminded of the other story Gerda had told, the one that teased at kisses and confessions behind a curtain of modesty.

Helvig shucked off her heavy coat and yanked her gloves off in her teeth with a little more vehemence than was strictly necessary.

"You didn't tell me about your princess," she said, and immediately hated herself for it. Jealousy bloomed from the words like blood from a wound.

Gerda didn't seem disturbed. She continued her long, luxurious strokes.

"You never asked."

"You were very bold. To just say, outright…"

"What? That I loved her?" She fixed Helvig with her pale eyes, shameless as the virgin in the manger. "That we passed the time as lovers do, with smiles and sighs and touches?"

"The men—"

"Hang what they think, or what they say. I cannot be bothered to care."

Gerda turned back to her work and silence crashed down between them. Helvig stood clenching and unclenching her hands at her sides, heart pounding like she had just raced Wilhelm to the nearest river and back.

She wanted….she didn't know what she wanted.

After a moment, Gerda spoke, her voice the rustle of dead leaves.

"You didn't tell me about her, either."

"Who?"

"Whatever girl you see when you look at me. The one who made you so afraid to speak kindly to or touch another woman."

Astrid's name sat like a stone in the pit of Helvig's stomach. The heaviness of it pained her, and so did the knowledge that she had carried that name for three years now, all the while drinking deep from the bitter cup of her own guilt.

Still, she did not give the name over to Gerda.

The witch finished her work and put her comb down on the floor with a definitive click.

"I see."

She was obviously disappointed by Helvig's silence, and the thief felt angry with her for that. How could Gerda deny Helvig her secrets when she had harbored her own for so long?

But then reason returned to Helvig. The only thing Gerda did not freely give of herself to anyone who asked were her secrets. She had earned the right to that much, in her long years of suffering.

"I should get to bed," Gerda said. She had her back turned to Helvig, and her shoulders were harshly squared. "It's sure to be a long day tomorrow."

"How do you mean?"

"You and your family have been very hospitable to me during these last few weeks. I don't wish to wear out your welcome, and now that you've heard my story, you understand why I must keep going. My brother needs me."

Helvig moved quickly to sit at Gerda's side. She was desperate to keep her but didn't know how. What could she possibly say that would outweigh a brother lost to the wilds of the north, or at least believed to be?

Her father's words, wary and wise, played over in her head.

I fear it's driven her mad.

Helvig had never known her father to be wrong, but she also had a hard time believing Gerda was mad. Misguided, perhaps, fixated on a hope she needed to give up. But not mad.

Helvig took Gerda's hand between her own. Her bones were so thin, but Helvig knew the strength beneath her skin. When Helvig had first met Gerda, she had wanted to protect her. Now she saw that Gerda was perfectly capable of protecting herself, and had been doing so for a very long time, but Helvig still wanted to care for her, if only to give Gerda a few moments of well-earned rest.

She could not lose this magnificent creature now, when her valor and cunning were on such brilliant display and she had finally decided to share the truth of her quest.

"I'm so sorry about your brother. I didn't know."

Gerda smiled tiredly. How many times she had received such condolences?

"Thank you."

Helvig wished desperately to give her greater comfort, but she had nothing else left to say. So, she darted in and kissed Gerda's cool cheek, a firm, closed-lip kiss of fidelity.

Gerda accepted the token with a courteous smile, but she also tilted her face into the touch, exposing her creamy white throat. Helvig's lips buzzed when she pulled away.

"Gerda," she began, placing her words down as carefully as she would her feet on a frozen lake. Her head was swimming with the memory of Gerda's skin, but she willed herself to speak plainly. "Do you think it's possible that maybe...that is...how can you be sure that Kai is alive, after all these years?"

Gerda's thumb swiped over Helvig's knuckles in a soothing, circular motion. The touch sent warmth spreading all the way up her arm.

Gerda shifted in a little closer, until their hips and knees were touching.

"There were many times I lost faith. But then I would hear Kai's voice in a dream or hear a dark story whispered in a tavern. Or a little child would tell me how they had seen the Snow Queen outside their window just the night before, and I was emboldened. I just...I know he's alive, Helvig. I feel it in my body as strongly as my own heartbeat. If he had died, a piece of me would have gone with him."

Ideas came together in Helvig's mind, slow and deliberate as tributaries feeding into a river. A tremor of excitement ran through her, and Gerda must have felt it too, for she held Helvig's hand a little tighter.

Gerda looked startled but hopeful, as though something wonderful and long-expected might finally happen to her.

"What is it?" she asked, leaning in even closer. They were so near to each other now. Helvig's chest was tight with fear and desire. Still, she would not let herself shatter the tenuous trust between them with an indiscretion.

She tore her eyes from Gerda's mouth and pressed another hard kiss to her temple, breathing in the scent of cedar in her hair.

Then Helvig was back on her feet, already a safe three steps away from Gerda so her hands and mouth couldn't wander.

"Get dressed. I've got a surprise for you."

Gerda blinked delirium from her eyes.

"Oh? Another present?"

Helvig peeked out the tent flap to ensure that her father had retired, and that the boys were otherwise distracted.

"No. Something better." She gave Gerda her best rakish grin, the one that only came out in moments of thrilled cocksureness."Something...darker."

TEN

Helvig wasn't sure how long the little church had stood abandoned in the middle of the woods. The building was squat and wood-shingled, with a rusty gate hanging cockeyed from the meager perimeter fence. Part of the roof had caved in from the weight of one too many snowstorms, and the parts of the roof left standing were covered in a layer of snow so thick it looked like gingerbread frosting.

"They say the midnight mass is held for those who died in the last year and never entered into heaven or hell. Or purgatory, if the Catholics are right," Helvig said. The deafening midwinter quiet made her feel as though she should whisper. "They say God allows the shades one night a year to gather, to read the scriptures and confess and prepare their hearts to cross over from this world to the next. Some find absolution. Others choose to stay."

When Helvig had told Gerda that she might know of a way to divine whether her brother was still alive, Gerda had leapt at the chance. She had learned many methods of divination in her time as a witch's apprentice, she said. She knew how to read candlewax dropped into water for news of upcoming marriages, and she could discern the sex of a baby from the splash of a mother's milk, but nothing had proved sufficient in revealing anything about Kai to her outside of vague platitudes.

"It will only work if Kai died in this region, and only in the last year, but if you're sure you tracked him up here..."

"I'm positive."

Gerda had brought Svíčka along, despite Helvig's reminder that it was likely to make noise and spook the ghosts. Now the crow shifted constantly on her shoulder and stretched its wings out before folding them in again. It was a strange thing for a bird to do, and Helvig wondered if it was feeling nervous.

Gerda certainly was, despite her calm exterior, or else she wouldn't have insisted on bringing along her feathered companion.

"Then the crowd will reveal whether or not he's alive," Helvig said. "I've heard sometimes spirits are more likely to show up if someone who loves them is nearby."

Gerda took a step towards the church, her new boots crunching through the snow, and Helvig's hand shot out to grasp her wrist.

Gerda turned to face her, and they were suddenly very close, close enough that Helvig could see the tiny snow shavings that had gotten caught in Gerda's eyelashes. The glow of the lantern gave both of their faces an eerie cast.

"What?" The witch asked, shifting even closer.

Helvig took a shuddering breath, the air pooling in clouds around her mouth.

"Mind your step in there. If you aren't careful, they will catch the fresh scent of you and fly into a rage. Ghosts cannot abide the presence of the living, not tonight of all nights. This night belongs to them."

Gerda quirked a fair eyebrow. Snow was gathering in a brittle tiara on her head. "You don't think I've seen my fair share of ghosts? We're haunted things, you and I."

Helvig felt a powerful urge to go down onto her knee into the snow. She wanted to pull off Gerda's glove with her teeth and kiss her perfect, cold fingertips, to press her mouth to the softness of her wrist and feel blood rushing through underneath.

Instead she reached up and brushed the icy crown away, as quick and casual as if she were wiping a smudge of dirt off Rasmus' forehead.

"Better haunted than haunting. I won't carry your corpse all the way back home through the snow, so if you want a proper burial sometime in your life, you had better be careful."

"I'll try to keep your inconvenience to a minimum."

Without another word, Gerda took the lantern from Helvig and turned towards the iron gate. She nuzzled her darling bird with her cheek and made a clicking sound that sent Svíčka winging up into the air.

The crow wound a tight circle in the sky, so dark against the night that it almost disappeared, and then came to rest on the church's decaying roof. Svíčka scuffled around as though she stood on untrustworthy, shifting ground, and let out an ear-splitting cry.

Helvig winced.

"That bird's going to give us away. Why is she acting like that?"

Gerda glanced back at Helvig, a wise smile playing at her lips.

"Birds are cleverer than people are, and crows always know when the dead are nearby. She's been trained for far more than looking pretty and doing tricks for morsels. She'll act as sentry, and the dead won't mind her."

Gerda's feet left a trail of dark prints behind her in the snow as she slipped through the crooked gate. She climbed the steps to the door of the church and paused, casting one last wary glance over her shoulder. Helvig wanted to rush up the steps to her, to throw an arm around her shoulders and deliver her into safety. But before she could say anything, Gerda had disappeared into the ecclesiastical darkness.

Helvig trotted along the side of the building, looking for a vantage point from which to spy the proceedings. She was grateful for the swollen moon casting silvery light down onto the clearing, but navigating in a midwinter night still wasn't easy.

She did not dare to set foot within the fence and avoided the front gate by a safe couple of feet. She knew a boundary line when she saw one, no matter how flimsy this one may appear.

A window that had been knocked out just above her eye level beckoned. She dragged over a hefty fallen branch, almost thick as a tree stump, and stood balanced on it to see inside.

The church was an open sore of emptiness, stripped of any adornment by thieves and weather. Thin wooden pews stood at attention facing a rudimentary altar. The ground was littered with fallen leaves and drifts of snow that had settled in through the open roof.

Gerda's skirts dragged behind her across the floor, audible in the perfect quiet of the church. No mice rustled around in the walls and no birds cooed at each other from the rafters. Even Svíčka had gone still on the roof, and Helvig wondered if the crow really was watching for ghosts with those keen, beady eyes.

The place had a patient, receptive stillness about it, a silence that felt too much to Helvig like an open grave waiting to be filled. She wondered idly if bringing Gerda out here was the best idea. She had heard enough stories about this church to know that real danger may wait for them on this night, but she also knew that without a strong conviction that there was no Kai left to search for, Gerda would scour the ends of the earth for him until the soles of her boots wore out and her hair turned grey.

Helvig held her breath as Gerda settled herself in one of the pews near the back of the church. No banshee cry split the air, no phantoms appeared to drag her by the hair out through the front door. So far, Gerda was proving the stories wrong, and Helvig very much hoped she could keep it up.

Helvig shifted on the log beneath her feet as Gerda glanced around the church, examining every eave for signs of the dead. Helvig sensed nothing ominous besides the feeling that the longer they stayed out here, the more likely her father was to find out that she had disobeyed him.

Gerda gripped the pew on either side of her with pale fingers.

"Just how long do we have to wait?" She asked.

As soon as Helvig opened her mouth to say that she didn't know, that the stories never specified, Svíčka began to caw on the roof. She cried out over and over again, letting loose ear-splitting sounds that made the muscles in Helvig's stomach clench. Undeniably, this was an alarm.

Despite her fear, Helvig couldn't help but marvel. She would have to try teaching Bae to sniff out gold, or to stamp with his feet whenever caravans heavy-laden with costly merchandise were nearby.

Helvig pressed herself against the wall of the church, trying to take up as little space as possible. She hoped she would not have to wait much longer, but just as Svíčka's warning cries were starting to grate on her, the fresh dead of the last year began to arrive.

At first, they were simply the suggestions of shapes between the trees, a slow-moving sense that something was not quite right. In the stories, ghosts were always spry and effervescent, but Helvig knew better. She knew the heaviness of the dead, the way foreboding dragged at her heart whenever they were near. It wasn't that she had seen many in her life, nor that she considered herself any kind of medium. But Gerda had been right when she had called Helvig haunted. No matter where Helvig pitched her tent, or how far away she ran from the sins of her past, Astrid always found her. You couldn't escape a ghost when it lived inside your head.

"Put out the light!" Helvig hissed.

Gerda swung open the lantern's glass hatch and blew out the flame inside. She returned her hands to her lap, her movements so tiny that her clothes hardly made a sound, and sat in statuesque stillness. Svíčka's cries had abated, but the crow still skittered along the roof and clucked to herself nervously.

Now, harbingering dread settled into Helvig, colder than the cruelest winter. The trees beside her stirred though there was no wind, and the distant crunch of snow beneath unseen feet grew closer and closer. The only comfort she had in this horrible situation was that Astrid, with her goldenrod hair and her brown eyes so full of hate, had been dead for a very long time. She would not be in attendance at this night's mass, having already crossed over to whatever nether world had opened its arms to her years ago.

The church's iron gate swung open of its own accord. The heavy presences swirling through the forest coalesced into figures as clearly outlined as Helvig's own hands. They came from all directions, emerging from footpaths and stepping fully formed from forest blackness.

When she glanced from the corners of her eyes, she clearly saw singular figures dragging legs behind them, or couples walking arm in arm, or tiny children reaching out to grip at the cloak of whoever was near them. But when she looked right at them, faces faded to vague desolation and the ghosts lost their substance. It was only through the accidental glance that she could see the details of their clothes, the bullet holes in their breasts, the rictuses of mortal pain scrawled across their faces.

An old man with a gnarled beard and a pilgrim's cloak so tattered it looked like it had been lifted out of a tale of Thor's bravery brushed past her. *Really* brushed, so much that Helvig was gently jostled. Sickly dread shot through her.

There were all so impossibly real. Helvig felt like she was the one back from the dead and trespassing on holy ground as she watched the ghosts silently march towards their day of holy obligation.

She tore her eyes away from the ghosts filing in through the door and peered in through the gloom to where Gerda sat motionless. It was more difficult to see now that the lantern had been extinguished, but the moonlight spilling in through the decayed roof afforded Helvig light enough while her eyes took their time adjusting.

The dead took their seats as though they had been assigned, slipping down the aisles and settling themselves in beside the living girl who had stolen into their midst.

Gerda, somehow, kept her head. Helvig didn't think she could look any paler, and her chest was rising and falling with shallow, quick breaths, but she didn't shriek, didn't squirm or bolt. Occasionally she would incline her head and let her eyes glide across the room, searching for her lost brother's face, before staring straight ahead again.

Helvig, who had grown up watching men play stabscotch and pick the purses right off town constables, had never seen someone so brave.

The trickle of lost lives was slowing now as fewer plague victims and prisoners of war appeared out of the forest. Helvig's heart hammered fast in her chest. She prayed that soon, this would all be over, and Gerda would see that her brother had died in the harsh north, and she could finally find her peace. Then they would go home together and warm each other in bed and talk of more hopeful things.

The thief peered into the church, looking for someone who matched Kai's description. There were boys here, little ones and ones on the cusp of manhood, but none, she realized, that fit Kai's description. He would be fifteen now, and Gerda had said that Kai was as fair as her. The only boys of proper age were a pair of twins with brown skin, darker than Helvig's, and tightly coiled hair.

Through the dim of the ancient church, Gerda met Helvig's eyes. She shook her head, almost imperceptibly.

He wasn't there.

As the final churchgoers arrived, the door swung shut of its own accord, making Gerda start.

The priest began making his way down the center aisle with lethargic, labored movements. In some moments his vestments looked brilliant and new, in others tattered and gnawed by worms, and he clutched a leather-bound book tightly to his chest. He took each step towards the front of the church as though it pained him, and as he passed through a shaft of moonlight, Helvig saw that his face was blue and bloated, caught forever in the moment of drowning.

He turned to face his congregation, raised his arms, and everyone rose to their feet.

Everyone except Gerda.

She blinked as though roused from a dream and shot quickly to her feet, but she was out of synch with the rest of the church. The priest held his hands above his head for a moment, ready to begin his sermon, but then he put them down.

Helvig's heart turned over in her chest. Wrong. Something was wrong.

The priest clasped his hands over his middle, very sorry to have to do whatever it was he was about to do, and then his doughy face lolled to one side.

His eyes fell on Gerda.

The blood froze in Helvig's veins.

"No," she whispered.

Gerda staggered, the weight of the priest's stare nearly bowling her over. To be so seen in a place like this, and by things that no mortal eyes were ever meant to perceive, had rattled her ironclad resolve.

She picked up her skirts and excused herself silently, pressing past the ghost of the old woman who had sat down beside her. Every face in the room followed her, and the irritated hum of voices and clearing of throats began to echo through the tiny church.

The ghosts shifted restlessly, turning to watch Gerda go. Some of them stepped out of their pews.

"No," Helvig repeated, terror squeezing her heart in a vise. If anything happened to Gerda, she would never forgive herself.

She hopped off her log and began to walk briskly in time with Gerda outside the church, glancing through every broken window and gaping hole in the wood to get a glimpse of what was happening inside. To her horror, the shades were following Gerda, slowly at first but then with a vigor the dead had no businesses possessing.

Helvig resisted the urge to dash inside and pull Gerda to safety, or to yell for her get out of there. Any sounds she made now and any action she took could topple the knife's edge balance between life and death inside the church, and break whatever spell was keeping the ghosts from taking full, terrible notice of Gerda.

The murmuring grew to grumbling, the cleared throats to territorial growls.

Gerda stepped faster and faster across the floorboards, somehow resisting the temptation to break into a run. Her beautiful face was ashen with terror, and her lips were pressed tightly together to keep from screaming.

Then, one of the dead children reached out and grabbed for the hem of Gerda's dress.

She shrieked as she pulled away.

The enchantment fell apart.

The dead lunged forward in a unified wave, scrambling over each other and crawling across the pews to get at her. The young and the old, women and children, all clawed at her skin and tried to seize her dress. It was like a nightmare Helvig couldn't wake up from, and ten times worse than the dreams in which only she suffered, and not her dear friend.

She hooked her fingers into a chasm that was once a window and hoisted herself up, ready to crawl inside the belly of hell if it meant she had a chance of saving Gerda. But the witch had managed to shake her assailants off and was sprinting blindly for the door and for freedom.

Helvig pushed herself off the wall and fell heavily into the snow, but she was up in a flash. With all pretenses at stealth gone, she tore around the building shouting Gerda's name. Svíčka had taken flight and was screamingly wildly, swooping low over Helvig's head.

Helvig turned the corner just in time to see Gerda burst through the front door. The moonlight caught her contorted expression. She was so terrified she hardly looked like herself.

To Helvig's horror, the ghosts followed, still raising unearthly cries as they squeezed through the door three at a time. Svíčka dashed in erratically to peck at faces or hands, but they seemed not to feel any pain. They were driven forward by a blind, wild need unlike anything Helvig had even seen before, not even in starving animals or men staring down a death sentence.

Gerda skidded down the steps, landing on her hands and knees. She scrambled forward in the dark and Helvig knew that if she didn't make it back through the same gate she had entered from, she was worse than dead. Helvig didn't know her lore as well as Wilhelm, but she understood the idea of spirit gates, and the landmarks that acted as tenuous barriers between this life and the next.

"Run, Gerda, run! The gate!"

Gerda was mere feet away from safety when a ghost who looked like he could have been a blacksmith during his earthly life seized hold of her cloak. He dragged her backwards, and her scream came out choked. She had only seconds before she was overtaken entirely.

Helvig burst through the gate, throwing out an elbow to knock away a burn victim who lunged at her. She grabbed the nearest part of Gerda she could reach, which happened to be her ankles, and started dragging her back towards the gate with all her might.

For an awful instant Gerda looked like she may be torn in two by the opposing forces vying for her life, but then she fumbled with the clasp of her cloak until finally it came free.

Her beautiful fur flew backwards into the mass of attackers, who shredded it to pieces.

Gerda stumbled through the mouth of the gate, wheezing like she was on her deathbed. She couldn't stay on her feet for more than a moment, and Helvig sank down with her into the snow as she fell. Snow bled through the knees of her breeches, but she didn't care about the cold or the wet so long as Gerda was alive.

Helvig cupped Gerda's face in her hands, terrified by her rolling eyes and gasping breaths.

"Are you alright? Gerda, tell me you're alright, please."

Svíčka landed in the snow beside them. She took up a bunch of Gerda's hair in her beak and gave a frantic tug, trying to wake her.

It took the witch a moment to catch her breath, but then her eyes refocused and she clutched Helvig's hands.

"I'm fine," she panted, already pulling herself to her feet. "We need to keep moving, they're—"

Her voice died as she glanced fearfully over Helvig's shoulder, and the thief followed her gaze. What she saw staggered her even more than the ghosts who had so dutifully filed into their pews.

The churchyard was empty. The old gate hung harmlessly on its frame as though it had not, moments ago, permitted a human girl access to the realm of the dead.

There was no evidence of her struggle except a little mound of kicked-up snow and a strip of tattered white fox fur.

Gerda shivered, either from fear or from cold, and Helvig shucked off her boxy outer jacket. The night was mercilessly cold, but she had more layers to spare than Gerda, and she would happily walk home with a chill in her bones if it meant Gerda could keep warm.

"Where did they go?" Gerda whispered as Helvig draped the jacket over her. Her shoulders were trembling, and Helvig smoothed her palms across them and gave a reassuring squeeze.

"I don't think that's for mortal minds to know. Come on. Let's get away from this terrible place."

Gerda turned around and sagged into Helvig's arms, and the thief crushed her in a tight embrace. Helvig held her until they were breathing as one, their faces buried in each other's necks, and until Gerda had stopped shaking.

"We'll sneak back into the tent and get as warm as we can," Helvig murmured. "And we'll get some proper sleep. I promise you I'll steal you a new cloak Gerda, even more luxurious than the one you had before. Or I'll make one, from finest stoat and rabbit, so soft you can hardly believe."

The witch's body had just begun to soften against Helvig's own, but now she straightened. Helvig trailed off, abandoning her dreamy reverie.

Something wasn't right.

Gerda scooped Svíčka up out of the snow and cuddled the small bundle of bird to her chest. Her face was so solemnly resolute it could have been carved from ice.

A light in Helvig's heart flickered out.

"Kai's still alive," Gerda said. "I have to go north."

ELEVEN

"You can't just go charging up into the ice at this time of year with no caravan to protect you," Helvig huffed, kicking up snow as she rushed to keep up with Gerda. The witch was pushing through the forest with dogged determination, pressing fir branches forward and almost hitting Helvig with them when they flew back. "It's suicide!"

"I can't stay here another day knowing that Kai is alive," Gerda responded, out of breath from her exertions. They had set off from the church at a ferocious pace and she had no intention of slowing. She had put Svíčka back on her shoulder, and the bird was bobbing its face in and out of her curtain of hair as though it were a game.

"What about trolls, imps, the ghosts? The days between Christ's mass and Epiphany belong to them. You think what happened to you in that church was scary? You haven't seen anything in these woods yet, girl."

"I'm alive, aren't I? I'll be able to manage for a few days more."

The encampment was up ahead, a few dwindling cooking fires casting an orange glow on the trees. Gerda burst through the tree line and marched towards Helvig's tent, head tucked down against the wind. Her hands were stuffed deep in her fur muff, and her skirts swirled around her in the snow.

She was leaving, Helvig realized. This may be the last time they ever saw each other. All without Helvig ever having the chance to say everything she wanted to.

Gerda ducked into the patch of trees where Bae slept soundly, and cupped Svíčka in her hands. Murmuring softly, she stroked her feathered head with her little finger, eyes full of motherly concern. She was acting like Helvig wasn't even there.

"This is madness," Helvig said. She was loitering at the edge of the trees, numb from the cold and from the blow of Gerda's sudden departure. She was really going to lose her, and just as they had begun to grow close.

Gerda carried on coddling her pet, kissing her tiny head like she was never going to see her again. But of course, it was Helvig she was abandoning, Helvig who she had taken up for a time as a charming diversion and now felt perfectly comfortable casting aside.

"For God's sake at least look at me," Helvig said. Her body had developed a keen skill for turning fear into anger during her life as a highwayman, since anger was more useful in a fight. A familiar, jittery rage seeped into her blood now.

Gerda placed Svíčka delicately in the boughs of her preferred tree, and then brushed past Helvig towards the tent, hardly meeting her eyes.

"I know what I'm doing," she said in her papery wise-woman voice.

"You're being stupid," Helvig blustered, darting into the tent after Gerda. "I won't let you go."

Gerda spun to face her, defiance in her eyes. Helvig was surprised by her aggression and took a faltering step backwards.

"Won't you?" Gerda demanded. "Will you walk off into the ice and white with me, then, not sure what will be waiting for us on the other end? Defy your father and abandon the men who answer to you? I think not."

Helvig's lips burned. She remembered one of Wilhelm's longwinded stories, about an angel pressing a fiery coal to the lips of one of God's chosen and commanding him to prophesy.

She felt sure that whatever words passed her lips next would be just as true, but like the prophecies in Wilhelm's good book, she feared her truth had the power to destroy lives.

"I would follow you down to death if you asked me. Just to make sure the Devil didn't have his way with you."

Gerda huffed. She did not appear to be impressed.

"That would be a very poor use of your time. I assure you I'm not worth the effort."

"Gerda." Helvig's tongue was heavy with words unspoken. "You're my...you're the finest girl I've ever known. You must know that by now."

The witch gave her a pitying glance. She was kneeling by Helvig's bed, tucking her few meager possessions back into the leather bags she had carried them in when she arrived.

"I know, Helvig. And I'm all the sorrier for that. But I promise you I am quite forgettable. You should love this free life here in the woods, and not worry about me."

She turned away, rolling up her few items and stuffing her bags with them. Helvig couldn't stand to watch. She had hoped their trip to the church would delay Gerda, maybe even convince her to give up her search entirely. Instead, it had only stoked the furnace of her devotion to her brother.

Helvig knelt in front of Gerda and clasped her hands so they couldn't put anything else away.

"Listen to me," she said, voice hoarse. She fixed Gerda with her most sincere look, squeezing the girl's hands to keep her own from trembling. "I may not be a real princess, but I can love you just as well as one. If it's a beautiful maiden you want, I'll braid up my hair and wear skirts and sweet perfumes, and if you tire of that and want a dashing prince, I'll be that, too. I'll steal you bottles of sherry and dresses of every color and sapphires big as your eyes. I'll lay my spoils at your feet and let you drink from my cup. God, Gerda, I've only known you a little while but I'm so...ust stay with me, and you'll want for nothing. I'll learn to be good, and sweet, and polite, I promise."

Gerda brought one hand up to cup Helvig's cheek. Helvig couldn't decide if Gerda was trying not to smile or trying not to cry.

"I wouldn't want you sweet, or polite. I like you just as you are, wild and forthright, and I already think you're better than good. But I can't stay."

She leaned in to kiss Helvig's cheek, a soft, lingering kiss that was much closer to Helvig's mouth than was strictly necessary. The thief bit back a groan of agony and pleasure, her emotions whipping themselves into a maelstrom inside her chest.

Why couldn't she feel something that was the right size, for once? Why not just a little bit of disappointment, or a manageable twinge of desire? Why did she have to be overcome with devastating, abasing affection whenever Gerda looked at her with all that pale fire in her eyes?

It wasn't fair. Other girls didn't have to learn how to manage all of these emotions for the friends who plaited their hair or slept in their beds. Other girls didn't have appetites that terrorized families and brought ruin down on whole towns.

"He could still be dead, you know," Helvig said. "If he died in another region his ghost would be attending another mass, probably. Or he could have already moved on. One slim chance of finding him isn't worth your life."

"He wouldn't. He would have waited for me. I'll still take my chances, for Kai's sake."

Helvig felt wicked for thinking so, but oh, how she wished Kai really was dead, in a grave that Gerda could visit and weep over and adorn with cowslips and daisies. Not because she wished any ill on an innocent boy, but so Gerda could be free of this obsession that was wearing her thinner and thinner every month she spent out on the roads calling his name. True mourning would not be pretty, Helvig knew, and Gerda might withdraw into herself and close her heart off to outsiders, despite their best intentions. But Helvig was willing to accept that if it meant she was nearby to take care of Gerda in her grief, to cook her fresh venison and bandage her feet and make her smile with wicked tales, if only every once in a while.

But this was selfish fantasy. Gerda would never stay unless coerced, and Helvig had promised to do her best not to wheedle or force Gerda's choices. She should be ashamed of herself for wanting to see Gerda so miserable that she needed Helvig to care for her. She had to let go.

But not tonight. It was too soon, too unexpected. She needed tonight at least to say goodbye.

"Gerda, it's pitch-black out there with snow up to your knees. Pass one more night with me, I beg of you. In the morning I will send you on your way with food and water and the kindest encouragement." Her voice wavered. "Would it be so terrible to spend one more night in my bed? How could one more night hurt anything at all?"

Gerda tipped her face towards heaven, her eyes shut tightly. Helvig had never seen her in so much pain, not even when she had tripped over a log while foraging with Wilhelm and come home limping on a sprained ankle.

"Do you remember the witch?"

Helvig blinked. The subject seemed incongruous to the issue at hand.

"From your stories? The one who taught you your art?"

"Yes."

Gerda pulled herself onto the bed and sat still for a moment, shoulders sagging. She looked a hundred years old, sitting like that.

"Come here, Helvig," Gerda said quietly.

Helvig sank down beside her and pulled one of her frail hands onto her knee. She was so cold, too cold, and a fresh wave of fear at releasing Gerda into the merciless weather passed through Helvig.

"I had already been travelling for over a year when I met her. I heard of a woman wise in the art of mending bones and curing heartache, so I offered to work as her household servant in exchange for being taught the secrets of her trade."

Gerda threaded her fingers through Helvig's own and averted her eyes. She was afraid, the thief realized. No. She was ashamed. But what in the world could clever, capable Gerda, who never wavered in her commitments, have to be ashamed of?

"And she accepted?" Helvig prompted tentatively.

"More than that. She took me into her arms like I was a long-lost daughter and opened her home to me. I was given my own bedroom, my own share of her dinner table. By day we would go out into the fields to harvest herbs, and by night she would tell me stories while I threaded her needles or wrote out her spells. I summered with her, then wintered. The next thing I realized I had been with her almost a full year. I had never intended to stay more than a month or two, but when I tried to remember how I had come across her house, or how long I had stayed, I found I couldn't recall. Events that happened only days before felt fuzzy, and events from weeks prior were barely any clearer than a dream."

Helvig's dark eyebrows knit together.

"I don't understand."

Gerda smiled wryly with tears glistening in her eyes. Irony, it seemed, did not dull the pain of what had happened.

"She mixed a forgetfulness draught into my tea every morning with a bit of blackberry jam. Another one of her spells. She was lonely, I gather, and didn't want me leaving her to go hunting for my brother."

Understanding settled in Helvig's stomach like sickness. In that moment she wanted terribly to run that old woman through with her knife, and the ferocity of the thought frightened her.

"Joseph and Mary, Gerda, I'm sorry. That's so awful."

Gerda shrugged.

"Life is like that. You want to know something grim? I can't part with that charm she made for me, even though I know what she did. Part of me still loves her, despite it."

"I don't think that's grim. You're allowed to love someone who also did wrong by you. That's just how hearts are, sometimes."

Gerda almost smiled, and her fingertips swirled across Helvig's skin with idle acquiescence.

"At any rate I learned my lesson. I let her distract me from Kai; I let her into my heart and my poor brother was left alone for another year because of it. So you see, no matter how much I may want to, I can't let that happen again."

"She drugged you, Gerda," Helvig said firmly. How long had Gerda been carrying this guilt inside herself? Triple swords of pity, anger, and admiration pierced Helvig's heart. "You had no choice."

"Didn't I?" Gerda swiped a dainty palm across her eyes, poised even as she cried. "All those lives I lived, all those people who brought me into their home and treated me as a sister or a daughter…they were moments of happiness I stole from the span of Kai's life. Every month I passed eating buttered bread with the tanner's son or telling stories by the fire with the witch was another month Kai spent trapped under the Snow Queen's spell. I have been so selfish, Helvig."

She circled her arms around Helvig's neck and hitched herself halfway onto her lap, holding back sobs that made her narrow frame shake. Helvig was stunned by her closeness, but she clung to Gerda all the same, letting her seek whatever comfort she could.

After a while, Gerda's tears ran out, but she stayed draped over Helvig, her slight body warming Helvig's through their clothes. Despite the plummeting temperatures outside, Helvig felt like she was burning up.

"You are the least selfish woman I have ever met", she said.

Gerda sniffled and daubed at her red eyes, giving a bitter laugh.

"I am no woman. I have become something else altogether, something cold-tempered and poisonous that still holds the shape of a girl."

"Really?" Helvig ran a light touch up Gerda's arm, over her narrow shoulder, and around the bow of her gosling neck. Her fingers shook as she slid them into the curtain of Gerda's hair and rested her palm on the peach fuzz at her nape. "You don't feel cold to me. You're warm as summer."

A smile touched Gerda's lips. She leaned into Helvig's touch, just barely, but enough to make the hair on the thief's arm stand on end.

"You think so?"

Gerda's face was perilously close. Helvig thought of Gerda's royal bedmate, and of Astrid, flushed and giggling in a field of wildflowers.

"Yes. And I don't think you're poison at all."

The tip of Gerda's nose brushed against Helvig's. A gentle nuzzle, unashamed as a foal seeking the comfort of its mother.

"No?"

"No," Helvig replied, with her breath already in Gerda's mouth. She drew the other woman to her, and the inch of safety between them disappeared.

Helvig kissed her, drinking in her warmth as though she was a prisoner of war who had been denied water for days on end. Gerda's hands were on her shoulders and then on either side of her face, tipping her chin up into sweet oblivion. Gerda tasted like sharp anise and melting ice, and when she sighed Helvig's name, Helvig was utterly and irredeemably lost.

A sigh of hitched breath, the rustle of skirts and fur, and they were reclining against each other on the bed.

This was worse than unsafe, this was tempting injustice and misfortune and all the other forces that had greedily eaten up the last girl that Helvig had let touch her like this. But it was so hard to stop. Gerda's narrow hips fit perfectly in her hands, and her lips were nimble across Helvig's skin.

"Astrid," Helvig gasped. "Her name was Astrid."

She didn't want to disrupt their embrace, but she knew that if she didn't tell her now, she would be sick with guilt no matter what came after. Gerda deserved to know. It was time.

Gerda pulled just far enough away to study Helvig's face, her blue eyes shining, her hair falling in a tangle.

"The girl in the story," Helvig went on, a bit sheepishly now that she was being stared at. "She and I—"

"I know." Gerda settled down on top of Helvig's chest, drawing a little design with her fingertip on the skin exposed by the open collar of Helvig's shirt. Pleasant goosebumps rose on Helvig's chest. "Or at least I guessed. But I didn't want to pry."

"Oh," Helvig said softly. Perhaps she had been foolish to think that Gerda wouldn't put the pieces together, sharp-minded as she was.

"I'm sorry she died," Gerda said. "You must have been heartbroken. If you still miss her, and don't want us to go on, I understand."

"No, it isn't that. Although I was miserable when it happened, and…I do still think about her sometimes."

"Of course you do," Gerda said, without jealousy or surprise. She seemed so worldly and wise about the subject of heartbreak, and Helvig very much wished she had more experience talking about these kinds of things.

Helvig rubbed slow circles into the back of Gerda's neck. It was easier to speak when she didn't have to look straight at her, when she could just feel her weight and her warmth instead. "I…I treated what we had as a dalliance, as a diverting way to pass the summer but she…"

"She thought you meant to keep her," Gerda said. She nodded, understanding instinctively, and a relief that Helvig hadn't expected washed over her. She had told so few people about what happened with Astrid: Rasmus, in gossiping whispers to help break the monotony of chores, and her father, tearfully while begging for him to help fix what she had broken. Neither of them had fully understood, though she was grateful for their willingness to listen.

She had always thought that telling the tale again would be hard and painful, an invitation for someone to see her as a spectacle.

"Yes," Helvig said. Her fingers drifted farther up, tentatively threading through Gerda's hair. "Truth be told, she had started to frighten me. She was horribly jealous and didn't like me talking to any other girls or boys in the street, and she would pull my hair when I displeased her. When I told her my family would be moving on with the turn of the seasons, she grew…horribly angry with me. Begged me to take her with me, screamed at me for lying to her. We were in her bedroom, and she started striking my chest with her fists. Her parents heard us and came upstairs to tear us apart. I hardly escaped the house without having the life beaten out of me, but her fate was worse."

"The wedding."

"The wedding. It was going to happen anyway, but I forced her parents' hand, I think."

"You blame yourself?"

Helvig tilted her head to see Gerda better, her fingers still running through all that blonde hair.

"Of course I do. I corrupted an innocent girl. I ruined her life."

Gerda traced the curve of Helvig's lips with one delicate finger. The sensation sent a jolt through Helvig's body, and she had never been so sure that Gerda was indeed a powerful witch in her own right.

"You can't corrupt someone just by touching them," Gerda said. "We corrupt ourselves, with the choices that we make, and I don't think yours were wrong."

Helvig thought of telling the rest of the story, of how her father had been forced to move the encampment for fear of the townspeople sniffing her out, of how he had kept a closer eye on her ever since then, and of how she still dreamed of Astrid, no matter how hard she tried to put her out of her mind.

But in this moment words failed, and Helvig knew that she and Gerda had a stronger understanding between them than any story could explain.

"Listen to me now," Gerda continued. "You didn't force anyone to do anything. That girl saw her own fate coming towards her like the gallows and she clung to you thinking you could save her from it. But here's the hard truth of these things; you couldn't."

"How could you know?"

"What power does a robber girl have to stop the marriage of an eligible young lady to a man who can provide for her what her parents cannot? She shouldn't have blamed you for showing her some happiness in the meanwhile. It wasn't your fault."

"But the storm, the baby…"

"It wasn't your fault." Gerda kissed her again and again, murmuring the words like an incantation. Helvig's hands curled tentatively around the curve of Gerda's waist, and then Gerda slid them up higher, to explore the swell of her small breasts. This was a pleasure so tender it was almost painful, and Helvig kissed Gerda deeply, forgetting all about Astrid and the ice storm and that awful guilt she had carried for three years. Gerda's nimble fingers worked at the buttons of Helvig's blouse, exposing flushed skin inch by precious inch. "It wasn't your fault."

Helvig lost herself in what followed, in the pleasure of hands on soft skin and red-bitten lips and quivering legs. Gerda kept repeating her spell until she could hardly form words at all, until the only sound that could pass her lips was Helvig's name, cried clear and desperate as a prayer.

TWELVE

Helvig woke early, so early that the sun had not yet completed its slow climb over the western hills. There was a warm, satisfied ache in her hips and arms, and her sleep had been sound and dreamless.

She rolled over and reached for Gerda, to pull the other woman's warmth in and fold herself around her.

Gerda was not in bed.

"Gerda?"

Drowsy and half-drunk from sleep, she did not initially register that she was alone in the tent. Then her head shot up off the pillow and she threw her eyes around the emptiness.

Helvig was out of bed like a bullet from a gun. She fumbled in the dark for her boots and breeches, every sound amplified by the hollow place in the room where Gerda should have been.

Helvig swore and gasped, tearing on her clothes while her heart pounded so fast she felt sure it was going to burst. She couldn't have left by herself in the middle of the night, not without saying goodbye. She would not have left like this, not after...

Helvig snatched up her knife and coat, almost tumbling headlong as she rushed for the door. Underneath her coat she wore a linen undershirt, far too thin for the weather. She barreled out into the snow without taking the time to find her tinderbox and light the lantern.

The wind keened and howled, but Helvig couldn't be bothered to care. She ran frantically from dwindling fire to dwindling fire, looking for Gerda in the meager light.

Helvig slammed into someone, the collision rattling her teeth. She instinctively swung at her assailant, but they battered away her flailing arms and seized her by the wrists.

"Helvig, it's me!"

Rasmus was tangled around her, his breath misting in front of her face. He had a guilty, wild look in his eyes, and though Helvig knew she must also look a fright, her response was instinctive.

"What's wrong?"

"It's Gerda. She—"

"Took off, I know. Did you see her?"

"Helvig, I tried to stop her, I'm sorry—"

"Where did she go, Rasmus?"

Helvig's voice sounded like she had been screaming for a whole day and night. She hated the desperation coursing through her veins, but there was no escaping it now. Without Gerda she was just a revenant, a half-living thing driven forward by pure need. Why had she left without saying goodbye, without letting Helvig load her up with proper supplies?

"I have to find her. Rasmus, I need...I have to..."

"Come with me."

Rasmus fisted his bony fingers into the shoulder of Helvig's jacket and began pulling her with him away from the glow of distant fires, towards the forgiving shadows of the tree line. They stumbled over each other but Helvig kept pace, her heart pounding against her ribs.

"She stole one of the horses," Rasmus said. "She wouldn't be deterred. I tried, Helvig, I even pulled my knife on her but I just, I couldn't. I couldn't cut her, not even when I was supposed to be standing guard at the stable."

It was hard to tell in the dark, but it sounded like Rasmus

was fighting a wet, treacherous knot in his throat. Part of Helvig wanted to knock him into the snow for letting Gerda get away, but something like affection won out over her vengeance.

She put one of her gloved hands on the back on his neck and squeezed as though she were soothing a whimpering dog.

"I know, Rasmus. It's alright. You did what you could. Where was she headed? To town?"

It seemed unlikely, but Helvig could hope. If Gerda had turned south to seek her fortune elsewhere, Helvig would be distraught, but at least she would know Gerda hadn't thrown her life away in the icy wilderness.

"No, she rode straight north. And if she doesn't let up on her speed, she'll exhaust the mare before she even reaches Samiland."

"Christ on the cross, she's going to freeze to death up there. I have to get Bae, I have to go after her—"

Helvig skidded to a stop as Rasmus pulled her through the trees and into a small clearing where Bae was awake and tied to a fir, chewing feed placidly from the bag hanging from his neck. Helvig was so surprised by the sight of him that she couldn't initially pull words together.

"You...When?"

"I saddled him up as soon as she had gone. I was coming to wake you."

The boy unhooked a patchwork bag from over his shoulder and thrust it into Helvig's arms. Inside she spied tinned meats and some strings of dried fish and a few parcels wrapped in kerchiefs that she suspected were hardtack bread. Rasmus had also included a tinderbox and two thick tallow candles which he had undoubtedly had to barter his own possessions to acquire.

"I couldn't see what all she was carrying, but it didn't look like much. You'll both need food. If you hurry you can catch up with her before she reaches Lapland, and you might be able to turn her around."

Helvig stared into the bag for a moment more, marveling

at his thoughtfulness. Fortune had made unlikely playmates of them by throwing two children of the same age into close quarters, and they had seen their fair share of rivalries, arguments, and scraps. Rasmus cheated at cards and teased her mercilessly, and Helvig was always haranguing him about his lies and threatening to turn him in to the army if he didn't get better at thieving. But somehow, when Helvig was at the end of her rope, Rasmus was always there, and she had thrown herself between his foolhardy actions and their consequences too many times to count.

Helvig didn't have siblings, but she supposed it must feel a little like this.

Helvig slung the bag over her shoulder and threw her arms around Rasmus. The boy made a surprised choking sound while she squeezed him. They were not a very affectionate pair, and Helvig was always more likely to dole out encouragement with a punch to the shoulder than with a gentle touch.

But after a moment, Rasmus put his arms around Helvig and hugged her tightly.

"Please don't die." He sounded young, and scared, but then he cleared his throat and spoke again with his usual cynicism. "Your father is already going to kill me for losing a horse and I don't want him to skin me alive first for sending you off to your death."

"Come with me."

"What?"

Helvig pulled away but kept her hands tight around his shoulders. Excited possibilities buzzed through her, heightened by emotion and the late hour.

"You already lost one horse, what's another? Come with me. We'll get Gerda and bring her back, and we'll be heroes."

Rasmus' eyes skittered around the forest. He did not look convinced.

I know you care for her," Helvig urged.

Rasmus smiled crookedly, never one to pass up an opportunity to quip even when his safety was precarious.

"Not as much as she cares for you."

"That doesn't matter. I don't want you taking the fall for this alone. Go get a horse. We'll leave together and we'll come back together."

Rasmus shook his head, pulling out of Helvig's grasp.

"I'd rather stay where there's food and a warm fire, thanks. No promises that I won't rat on you to old Bertie when he tickles me with his knife, though, so you had better do whatever you're going to do quick"

Helvig swung herself up onto Bae's sturdy back. He had been well-saddled and was ready for a long trek. In the trees above, Svíčka ruffled her feathers and watched them with sharp eyes. She seemed irritated to be woken from her slumber, and Helvig realized that Gerda must have left the crow on purpose. The girl was so attached to her bird that Helvig couldn't imagine her leaving it unless she believed Svíčka would be safer here than with Gerda, and that thought sent a chill down Helvig's spine.

"You *are* brave, Rasmus," she said, unfastening the feed bag from around Bae's neck. "I promise you I won't forget this."

"Live long enough to buy me a drink and I'll consider the debt repaid."

Helvig didn't waste any more time on sentimentality; it wasn't their way. She kicked Bae forward with a cry and the deer set off at a clip through the snow, leaving Rasmus to shiver alone in the forest.

Gerda was a fool to take the horse. They couldn't survive this weather without campfires and a pair of helping hands close by with a feed bag. The animal would valiantly make the sprint for an hour or two, then tire, lay down in the snow, and eventually die.

Helvig was furious with Gerda for having the audacity to go and get herself killed without so much as asking first.

Underneath that anger was a fear strong enough to curdle blood, the fear that Helvig would soon find the finest creature she had ever known dead in a snowdrift. Gerda could argue otherwise, but Helvig knew what was true. If you loved something too much, especially something girl-shaped, you were all but begging the whole host of nature to swoop down and pick its bones clean. Well-loved things must taste sweeter to wolves and frostbite and bears.

Bae plodded on against the biting wind as the sun rose wearily. Helvig rode with her fingers knotted into his mane, her mind a whirlwind of contradictions. She should not have touched Gerda; she should never have let her go. She should never have mentioned Astrid; she should have told Gerda the whole story on the first day. And again and again: *you should have never taken her to the church, stupid girl.*

Further out past the thickest part of the woods, the terrain became increasingly sparse and rocky. Little grew this far north besides hardy mosses and low-lying shrubbery that reindeer knew to root under the snow for. The breathtaking lakeside vistas, which Helvig so looked forward to on her trips with her father to trade with the Sami, were lost on her now.

Every tree that was not Gerda, every rocky outcropping and fallen boulder, was a weight around Helvig's heart. Each mile she travelled further from safety brought her further from hope, and every new mountain the brightening sun revealed reminded her just how wide and empty her world was, until she was sobbing into her hands, alone in the world with her poisonous heart.

Bae grazed underneath her, indifferent to her suffering.

A faint tremolo wafted towards Helvig on the wind, and she snatched her hands away from her face.

A voice.

Helvig kicked wildly at Bae, disrupting his breakfast, and urged him forward in the direction of the sound. He tottered down a rocky grade, pebbles scuttering around his hooves, and then Helvig's eyes fell on a slim girl petting the mane of an exhausted horse. She sang softly in Danish, shivering in the heavy snow.

Helvig was off Bae before he had come to a complete stop. She sprinted to Gerda so quickly that the witch hardly had time to notice her before Helvig took her by the arm.

Gerda spun around, knife drawn and pressed to Helvig's throat, but when she saw who had grabbed her, her expression didn't soften. Wind whipped Gerda's hair around her stony face, turning her into a fearsome troll-wife.

"What have you done?" Gerda fumed.

Helvig felt no fear, only an all-encompassing need to make Gerda understand what she had done to her, to feel that in the pit of her stomach the way Helvig felt it in hers.

So this is why she's never afraid of anything. This was what it was like, to be driven by a single-minded need, heedless of the consequences.

Helvig knocked the knife away and crushed her mouth against Gerda's like she could kiss the death out of her.

Gerda struggled and wrenched herself free. All the blood had rushed to her mouth, pulsating an angry red. It seemed to Helvig the only proof that Gerda was really alive, and not a dead thing strung along by her quest to find Kai.

"God, you're infuriating!" Gerda cried. She was almost shrieking, her hands curled into fists. "I deliberately left you where you would be safe. What have you done?"

"Me? What have I done? I could ask you the same, stupid girl!" Gerda flinched when Helvig insulted her, and the thief knew she would regret saying it later, but twin waves of relief and rage crashed over her, swallowing her self-control. "You could have died!"

"Go back to your father Helvig," the witch said, her stony mask fixed back into place. "He'll be missing you."

"Not without you."

Gerda, apparently done with their conversation, turned back to her horse and reached for the reins.

"Do you know what it's like," Helvig hissed between her teeth. "Watching some girl drag your heart behind her like a pet she's gotten tired of?"

Helvig took up Gerda's knife and turned it towards her

own chest, then wrapped Gerda's hands firmly around the hilt. The tip bit into the flesh between Helvig's breasts and she squeezed Gerda's wrist hard enough to bruise, but neither woman relented.

Gerda's blue eyes were placid as ever, two lakes that would not give back what they had drowned.

"You're being nonsensical," she said. "Now let me go."

Anger clawed its way up Helvig's throat.

"I ought to just cut it out and give it to you, for all the use I have for it. Maybe you can use it in one of your spells."

"If you stand in my way, I will show you just how awful my 'spells' can be."

"I don't want to stop you. I want to go with you."

Gerda tugged her hands free, taking the knife with her.

"I won't have it on my conscience if you die up here."

"No one is going to die," Helvig said, so sternly she sounded like her father. "And how do you think I feel? You went off alone without supplies, without saying goodbye, and you left that damn bird that loves you so much...What was I supposed to do?"

"Respect my wishes!"

"I have respected your wishes! I've respected your secrets and your obsessions and your love for your brother, and if you spurn me and never want to share my bed again, I'll respect that too. But when someone you care for puts their life in danger you go after them whether you respect them or not. You're acting...You're acting like someone who doesn't care whether she lives or dies."

It terrified her to even say it out loud, but this felt too much like a suicide mission.

Gerda's shoulders sagged, folding under the immense weight she had been holding up for years.

When she spoke again, the fight had gone out of her voice.

"I'm tired, Helvig. I have been travelling for so long and I have weathered much suffering in this life and all I want is to see my brother again. Then I can rest."

"Then take me with you," Helvig insisted. She wanted to reach for Gerda, to pull her in close again, but she resisted the urge. "Let me guard you in your rest and your waking. I can't..."

Her voice sounded close to breaking. Gerda's eyes flitted across her face, studying her distress.

"What is it?" Her voice was softer than it had been moments before, and she drifted a little closer to Helvig, drawn by an invisible force.

"I may not believe in priests and penitences, but I believe in sin. What happened to Astrid was my fault and it's mine to carry until the end of my days. If I let that happen again; if anything bad were to happen to you..."

"Oh, Helvig," Gerda huffed, part irritation, part irrepressible affection.

Slowly, her hands found Helvig's. Helvig brought them up to her mouth and kissed Gerda's hands delicately, as though too much passion may bruise her.

"If Kai really is alive," she pressed on. "I want you to find him. I've thought it over, and it's true. I want to help you any way I can, and if you want to send me away, I won't argue. But please, hear me. See me."

"See you?" Gerda breathed. "I always see you. Even when I don't want to, even when looking at you and all the things I could have if I stopped striving causes me pain, I see you."

Helvig fumbled inside her many layers of clothing for the charm Gerda had given her. She slipped it over Gerda's head, lifting her braids up so the herbs sat against her neck.

"You forgot it," Helvig said in a raw voice.

"No, I didn't. It was for you. To keep you safe"

"Then humor me and keep it on for a little while more. You can give it back to me once this is all over."

Gerda shuffled closer to Helvig until their two bodies were pressed together, a barricade against the cold.

Helvig let Gerda encircle her in her arms, and the biting wind tangled their hair together.

"I'm still cross at you for putting yourself in harm's way," Gerda said into the fur of Helvig's hood. Her narrow frame shivered. How long would she have lasted out here by herself? "But I'm glad you're here with me."

"Yes, well," Helvig said, trying to bring a little levity to the situation. "You stole a horse. I couldn't let you get away with it."

Gerda seemed now to remember what she had done. "Poor Rasmus. He spooks so easily."

"It was he who sent you up fresh food and a tinderbox, so you'll have to thank him properly when we return to my father's camp."

She hoped desperately that Gerda wouldn't protest, that she could still imagine surviving long enough to stop by camp as she travelled down south.

"If Kai's not there when we arrive," Gerda said, voice hollow with terror. "If we can't find him after all…I don't know what I'll do. What I'll become."

Helvig had never heard a sweeter sound than the word "we" on Gerda's lips. The emptiness that had threatened to engulf Helvig over the past few hours was transmuted into wonderful lightness, and she squeezed Gerda tighter.

"We'll find him. But for now, we must keep moving. There's a herding family who passes their winters a few miles north of here. A friend of my father's is among them; she'll feed us and give us a warm place to sleep."

Gerda tipped her face up and gave Helvig a tentative kiss. The touch surprised Helvig, but it was just as earnest as the kisses they had shared last night. Helvig leaned gently into the touch.

"I'm…not used to people coming after me when I slip away," Gerda said. "Thank you."

Helvig stole one more kiss, delirious with the knowledge that she was allowed, that she could do it without the skies falling down around her. Then she nuzzled her nose against Gerda's.

"I told you I would follow you into Hell. Now bundle up

and get back on that horse. It's a long, cold road to Rávdná's yet."

THIRTEEN

In the dark part of the year, the northern reaches of land received only a few scant hours of sunlight a day, and the light was fading fast by the time they reached the Sami camp. It felt to Helvig, as always, a wellspring of life in the middle of an inhospitable, if starkly beautiful, landscape. Women ducked in and out sturdy triangular *lavvus* wrapped in reindeer hide, carrying baskets of household goods and swapping gossip.

The reindeer grazed in a great, meandering herd nearby, rooting tough lichen up from under the snow and wandering as they pleased. The men checked their deer's hooves and horns, or deftly repaired fishing nets while sending little boys running off with messages for their mothers. The entire camp was a swirl of color and vivacity, well-provisioned for winter and unbothered by its presence.

A child bedecked in florid shades of blue and red cried out in a language Helvig only understood in pieces. She shouted back a greeting and then added, in her native tongue,

"Go find Rávdná! Tell her that her little squirrel has come."

The child shouted back what sounded like a taunting song, but one of his older sisters appeared to usher him back inside with a click of her tongue.

"Are you sure it's safe?" Gerda asked.

"How do you mean?"

"You've heard the stories. They say the Sami are rough people."

Helvig let out a belly laugh. "Rough people? You must be thinking of me and mine. The Sami are herders and craftspeople. The same family has been bringing their winter herds down this way since I was a little girl, and my father has always done honest business with them. I grew up playing with these children, taunting their reindeer, sharing their food. This is one of the safest places north of Stockholm."

Before Gerda could reply, a thickly built woman appeared out of one of the *lavvus*. She wore her silver-streaked mane in a swirl on top of her head, and her face was as wrinkled as paper that had been crunched up and smoothed out many times. She put her mittens on her hips as they approached, cheeks glowing red despite the biting cold.

"My long-lost god-niece has come to pay a visit! Are you still toting around that deer like a plaything?" She squinted over their shoulders to the horizon. "Where's Berthold?"

"Uh…" Helvig began.

Rávdná sucked her teeth. One flick of her eyes across Helvig's guilty face told the whole story.

"You've run off, then?"

"Yes," the thief admitted wearily.

"Got a good reason, do you?"

Helvig glanced to Gerda, who nodded.

"Yes, I think we do."

Please, don't send us back to my father, please.

Rávdná harrumphed and regarded them with a keen eye. Snow collected on the shoulders of her thick coat. When she spoke again, she addressed Gerda.

"Are you hungry, little one?"

"Yes, ma'am. Awfully so."

The old woman nodded and turned back towards her home.

"Well, give over your mounts to one of the children. I'll

fix you both a bite and then we can have time for stories. What do you say?"

Helvig swung off her horse, relief washing over her.

"Rávdná, that's one of the finest propositions I've heard all day."

The meal was served with the generosity customarily shown to visitors, with cured meats and blood sausages laid out next to clots of cheese. Scents of vinegar and dill mingled together in a way that made Helvig's stomach rumble. Such bounty in the middle of the year's most barren season. The sight of the meal nearly brought tears to her eyes as she sat cross-legged next to Gerda in Rávdná's smoky *lavvu*.

Gerda wrapped a piece of salted reindeer meat in thinbread and pushed it into her mouth with greasy fingers. Helvig grabbed a handful of the cloudberries laid out on a cloth and took a deep sip of the fragrant *guompa*, fermented reindeer milk brewed with angelica stem and roots. The flavor was strong and not easily acquired by those accustomed to the food of the South, but to Helvig it tasted like childhood, like tight hugs and crunching walks through the snow with other children to go visit reindeer.

Rávdná watched them eat in comfortable silence, hands folded across her lap, eyes hooded in the glow of the fire. Helvig knew her way. She would not press them for stories or explanations until their bellies were full and the warmth of the *lavvu* had permeated all the way down into their bones. But when she questioned them, there would be no hiding anything. Helvig hoped Gerda wouldn't try her usual evasive tactics on the old woman. Rávdná was keener than either of them would probably ever be.

When the girls had supped their fill and were starting to become drowsy from the creature comforts of fur and fireside and food, the old woman spoke.

"Your father would never let you travel so far north unaccompanied, no matter how capable you may be of the journey." Not an accusation, merely a statement. She may not know about Astrid, but she knew how Berthold had tightened his daughter's leash after one of her dalliances brought icy ruin down on a city. "What's happened that has you so disobedient?"

Helvig opened her mouth to apologize for dropping in unannounced, but Gerda spoke first. With gentleness and, to Helvig's relief, with honesty. "She was saving my life. I ran off into the wilderness alone and unprepared. I didn't know what I was doing."

Rávdná nodded. Helvig knew she was turning the story over in her mind like a ruby, inspecting it for imperfections and cracks.

"I took Bae out before it was light," Helvig continued. "I was going to turn her around but by the time I caught her we were closer to you than to my father. I couldn't leave her out here on her own."

"Affection and foolhardiness make natural bedfellows," Rávdná said. "You're lucky we had already moved down to the winter grazing lands, or else you would be miles and miles from the nearest herding family."

When Gerda had accepted Helvig's offer to travel with her, the thief had felt only elation. She realized now that she hadn't thought through all the ways their journey could go wrong.

"What is your business in Sapmi?" Rávdná asked Gerda, using her family's own word for their ancestral region. "Are you trying to get in touch with one of my kin?"

Gerda pressed a cloudberry between her lips and shook her head.

"I'm afraid not. I'm searching for someone you've probably never met, someone who took my brother away from me when we were only children. I intend to get him back." She gave Helvig a wary glance, and the thief nodded. Gerda's story sounded like madness, that much was true, but there was no use lying to Rávdná. She had not raised eight children and traded goods with men as wily as Helvig's father without learning how to tell when someone was keeping the whole story from her. "I seek the Snow Queen."

Rávdná inhaled slowly and leaned back in her seat. A ribbon of smoke rose up from the fire crackling between them, partially obscuring the old woman's face on its way up to the hole at the top of the *lavvu*. As far as Helvig could tell, she was thinking.

"Yes, I've heard the stories. We have our own names for the spirits that move in the dark, and our own stories about the lives they claim."

Drowsy from her full stomach and the crackling fire, Helvig shifted closer to Gerda and settled in for a tale. She could never get enough of Rávdná's stories, so different from the wives' tales and fables that got passed around her father's camp. Rávdná told her tales of how the world was made from the body of a reindeer: the rivers from its blood, the constellations from its shining eyes, and the sky from the broad expanse of its skull. She told her of Laib Olmai, the forest spirit who granted favor to hunters who pleased him and ill fortune to those who did not, and of how her husband had won her hand in marriage after asking no less than seven times.

"This land does not belong to the Sami alone, or to the Swedes or the Finns or the Rus with their sabers and military caravans. There are things in the hills older than me, older than my grandmother's grandmother. Spirits that couldn't be separated from the land any easier than you and I could be pulled out of our bodies."

"Ghosts?" Helvig asked.

"No, they were never human. But they meddle in human affairs, sometimes, descending upon travelers lost in brutal winter and making them into...something else. Something only half alive. I know men who have seen dead wives or friends stepping out to greet them from great gusts of snow. But these...creatures, they're false as black ice, and they aren't the people they once were. They've become part of the land, wild and capricious, and they act without conscience or compassion."

"And you think that the Snow Queen we've heard stories about might be one of these creatures?" Helvig asked.

"I didn't say that. But it's possible."

"Why do the spirits of winter take people over like that?" Gerda piped up.

Rávdná shrugged. "What does an old woman know? Winter is always hungry, child, and all it knows how to do is take. Perhaps they think, in a way, that they're saving them from a slow death, and it's true the poor souls do live on well past their years. But from what I've heard it's no life worth living."

Helvig and Gerda exchanged a glance. They were pushing puzzle pieces around, trying to fit them together into a shape that was just out of reach.

"Do the creatures ever take children?" Gerda asked.

Rávdná nodded.

"I've heard they travel as far as the cold winds blow them to haunt children's dreams, and then sometimes, the children go missing. We all have our tales. There must be some truth to them, underneath the fear."

Gerda fell quiet. She looked as though she was slipping out of her body, her mind pulled away into distant reaches that even Helvig couldn't fathom. Rávdná watched her quietly, patient as she had ever been. Helvig was convinced that her god-aunt could outwait a glacier gliding across the plain if she put her mind to it.

Finally, Gerda asked,"Do you know where we can find such a creature?"

Rávdná squinted at them both, dark eyes spry as ever.

"Now, why would I let you know where to go poking at spirits in the darkest part of the year? Helvig, your father would kill me if I let you come back to him with so much as a scratch on you."

Helvig jutted out her chin.

"I'm not a child anymore. I'm going to get scratched plenty in this life and I would rather it be from helping a friend than anything else."

The old woman gave a curmudgeonly huff, but her eyes shined with pride.

"I ought to fill your waterskins and send you right back down to your father."

"But?"

"But I know that sometimes things need doing, no matter what the ones who love us might think. I can tell by looking at the two of you that if I turned you around you would just sneak past when my back was turned, and I don't want you wandering further north without directions. I'll warn you, I'm no great expert on these matters. I keep to myself and I don't concern myself with the mysteries of the dead or their kin. But I've heard things."

The same child who had called out to Helvig when they had arrived galloped into the *lavvu*, blonde hair flying askew as he tossed himself down next to his grandmother. Rávdná pinched his cheek and gave him a piece of flatbread.

"There's an old fort just under half a day's ride north of here," she said. "If you spare the horse and reindeer, which I suggest. Some of the youths tell stories about hearing whispers or the sound of a woman's cries coming from inside, even though it's been abandoned many winters now. You may find what you're looking for there. But if you don't, you must promise to turn back. Neither of you have the skill to navigate Sapmi by yourselves. I would have to give up one of my own grandchildren to guide you, and that's not a sacrifice I'm willing to make."

The little boy lolled against Rávdná's lap, eyes growing heavy as he curled up beside her. She stroked his hair.

"Thank you," Gerda said. Sometime while Rávdná was speaking, she had slid her hand over to Helvig's. Now, she squeezed it tightly.

The old woman's eyes clouded over as she began to clean up dinner, stacking plates and gathering leftovers.

"Don't thank me yet. You might not like what you find up there. Sometimes, it's better to let the land keep what it takes."

Helvig and Gerda slept curled against each other under a pile of furs, their noses warmed by the embers of the dwindling fire. Rávdná and a few members of her ever-growing family slept nearby, mostly grandchildren too young to have begun their own households.

They had passed the evening after dinner with gossip and laughter, and Helvig's heart had swelled at the sight of old friends. She had been better warmed by Rávdná's food than by anything she had eaten in her father's camp for months, and the familiar bustle of children ducking in and out of the *lavvu* made her chuckle.

But she couldn't help but notice how distracted Gerda had seemed. The witch hardly spoke, and her eyes jumped towards every shadow or strange noise.

Helvig and Gerda had gone to bed quietly, without indulging any of the new affections growing between them, but Helvig held tight to Gerda while they drifted off, afraid they would be torn apart in the night.

Helvig woke in the middle of the night when Gerda jerked against her, whimpering.

"Gerda?" She whispered. Helvig blinked the sleep from her eyes and shook her companion gently. Nightmares.

Gerda's eyes flew open and she grasped blindly for Helvig, pulling her closer. She pressed against Helvig and buried her face in her chest.

"Gerda! What's wrong? What did you see?"

Helvig tried to keep her voice low. One of the boys sleeping nearby stirred but didn't wake.

"Kai," Gerda breathed, voice muffled by Helvig's shirtfront. "He was drowning. I couldn't reach him. He opened his mouth to call out for me, and the water..."

Helvig wrapped her fingers around the back of Gerda's head, massaging gently with her fingertips.

"What if I can't save him? What if I'm not strong enough? What if he's already dead and..."

"Shh," Helvig soothed. She fought to keep her own anxieties out of her voice. "You're just shaken up. You're the most courageous thing I've ever seen, and you'll have me by your side tomorrow. We'll get him, Gerda."

Gerda's shoulders shook, but her tears were silent. She had long ago learned to keep her grief to herself.

"Hush now," Helvig fretted, nuzzling her dear companion. Gerda still seemed half-asleep, and so vulnerable in her distress. "It was just a dream. We're going to find him. He's alright, Gerda. Let's go back to sleep."

Gradually, Gerda slipped back into unconsciousness. Outside, wind blew hard against the *lavvu*, wailing through the camp like a woman mourning her lost love.

Helvig pulled Gerda close and held her through the night.

FOURTEEN

Rávdná saw them off the next morning with a wholesome breakfast of dried fish and barley soup, and loaded them down with supplies and strict orders to return to camp before dark.

The sun reflected off the white landscape with piercing brilliance as Helvig and Gerda started their trek further into the mountains. Their animals moved slowly over the rocky terrain, stretching the modest journey into several hours.

For most of the ride, Gerda said little. Her eyes had a bruised look that told Helvig she hadn't gotten much sleep. Helvig couldn't imagine carrying all of that hope and anxiety towards an unknown location. Helvig would occasionally point out a landmark her god-aunt had told her stories about, or narrate the adjustments to course they should be making based on where the sun was in the sky, but conversation was sparse.

Eventually, Helvig couldn't help but address the issue at hand. She got chatty when she was nervous.

"How are we going to kill her when we find her?"

"Mm?" Gerda asked, pulled from her thoughts.

"The Snow Queen, or whatever the proper name for a creature like that is. How do we kill something made of ice?

You must have given this some consideration, in your years seeking vengeance."

Gerda became distracted, and her eyes darkened.

"Yes, I suppose I have."

"Is she like a troll that turns to stone in the sunlight? Or do we need to saw off her head like a draugr? I haven't got much but a couple knives and some rope and my wits."

Gerda gave Helvig a smile that would have been disarming if it wasn't so forced.

"Haven't you heard? I'm a powerful witch. I'll defeat her with my magic."

Helvig wasn't satisfied. She had seen Gerda's magic, and healing salves, rune talismans, and beguiling smiles seemed ineffectual against a creature animated by the spirits of ice and snow. Helvig still wasn't sure they were going to find any creature at all, or just an empty old fort with no secrets inside, but she liked to know the odds she was facing regardless.

Just as she was about to press Gerda for more insight into what sort of magic she had planned, the witch gave a little gasp.

"Look!"

The stone fort hunkered down over the horizon, casting a long and tilted shadow. Helvig had not been alive during a time when Sweden's borders didn't bleed out into contested lands. Skirmishes on canals and trade routes were common, and all-out war never died down long enough to be completely forgotten. In the wild swing between wartime and uneasy peace, things fell through the cracks. Rasmus wasn't the only boy to have disappeared from the front lines without anyone noticing, and a whole fort being abandoned to weather and ruin was well within the realm of possibility.

Originally built on the precipice of a vast lake, no doubt blue in the summer but now frozen over gray, the fort had sunk further into the ground over time until a quarter of the structure was swallowed up by earth and water. Exterior walls crumbled away, and doors hung half-ripped from their hinges. It was hard to say whether it had been built on a faulty foundation from the start, or if its disrepair was the product of war.

They closed the distance to the fort easily, encouraging the horse and reindeer to pick up speed despite the gales blowing puffs of snow across the plains. Helvig brought Bae to a stop near the entrance, by an alcove tucked away from the worst of the wind, and swung herself down off his back.

She craned her neck to scan the high-reaching expanse of stone and mortar, taking it all in. The ground beneath her feet was frozen. Ice had seeped from the fort, from the lake, from the ground, and pooled at the entrance.

"Not a very cozy place."

Gerda shivered.

"Not at all."

Helvig stamped tentatively on the ice, testing her weight. It was difficult to know where the ice stopped and ground began, and Helvig had seen men disappear under rushing water that looked frozen from above

"Seems solid enough to me."

Gerda followed gingerly, despite the fact that she weighed almost nothing. Helvig was much more likely to go down first, if either of them.

They entered through the askew door. Their footsteps were deafening in the stillness as they descended into darkness. Virtually no light penetrated the tiny slit windows high above their heads, and Helvig clutched Gerda's hand tight as they navigated carefully, wary not to slip and fall. The little huffs of Gerda's breaths on her neck reminded her that she was still very alive and not alone, despite the gloom of the fort.

"What are we looking for?" Helvig asked.

Gerda shuffled closer, feet crunching over soft ice and debris.

"I'm not sure. Any signs of habitation? Barring that, any evidence as to where Kai might have gone."

She already sounded skeptical. Helvig could not imagine what Gerda would do if this turned out to be another false lead. Despite the herculean perseverance she had shown in her search for Kai, Helvig didn't know how many dead ends Gerda had left in her.

"Look! Light, up ahead."

Gerda skittered forward, tugging Helvig through the dark towards the grey glow ahead. Through an archway, a central hall sprawled with half of its ceiling torn away to the sky, and the weak midwinter sun fell through the gaps along with snow.

The tilted angle of the whole structure meant that the girls had to half-hop, half slide down iced-over stairs to reach the hall, which sat at a much lower elevation than the door they had entered through. A thick flood of ice slathered the floor, bringing the ceiling of the great structure closer to Helvig's head and partially obscuring the stone supports that held up the building. Frozen waves rose up against the stone walls in whorls.

"It looks like someone tried to sink the fort," Helvig murmured. It was difficult to fight the instinct to whisper. There was something…wrong about the place that made her worried to be found there.

"Or raise the lake."

Here, the snow on the ground was so thick that Gerda's feet disappeared into it as she crunched into the center of the room. Helvig, who had been trained from a young age to mark her exits and watch for ambushes, scanned the corners of the room, any doors suitable for escape, and a narrow walkway running across the second floor.

She could see and hear nothing. But unmistakable dread trickled through her veins, the same dread that had washed over her in the churchyard moments before the ghosts had appeared. She had the awful sensation that she and Gerda were not alone in the fort, and that something was watching from the far edges of her perception.

"Something's off," Helvig said.

Gerda didn't turn to look at her. She was surveying the frozen lake with dead eyes, her mouth set into a grim line.

She looked a thousand years old.

"Do you feel that?" Helvig pressed. She sifted through words, trying to find ones that fit the cold weight in her chest. "It's…a presence. Heavy. Angry."

Gerda hardly seemed to have heard her. She buried her chin down into her scarf, hands hidden within her thick muff, and looked for all the world like a statue abandoned alone to gather snow. Her eyes burned behind glassy tears.

"Nothing living could have survived out here for more than a day," she said in a raw voice. "It's open to the elements and flooded out."

Helvig didn't realize she had drawn her knife until she saw herself gesture with it to the ground.

"Old forts often have storerooms below ground. If Kai was able to find light and water, he may be there still. He might have found some old rations."

She suggested this partially because it was possible, however improbable, and partially because she was gripped by the desire to get out of this room as quickly as possible. Despite the open ceiling, the air was fetid and hard to breathe.

"We'll have a look at the lower levels," she went on. "See what we find. You never know."

Gerda drifted towards Helvig, snow swirling around her feet like a trained pet. She seemed reluctant to leave this part of the building. Perhaps she had imagined having some final confrontation with her brother's kidnapper here or throwing her arms around poor imprisoned Kai.

Then, just as she turned to go, a sound like fingernails being dragged across ice echoed down from the second level of the building. Helvig's eyes snapped up in time to spy a wraith-thin silhouette in white. It slipped across her vision, taking three measured steps across the stone before disappearing into darkness.

Helvig seized Gerda's arm.

"Someone's here."

Gerda threw her eyes wildly up to the second level, her

breaths coming quick and shallow. Helvig realized then how unprepared they were for whatever might find them. Gerda knew medicine, and embroidery, and blacksmithing, and Helvig could throw a solid punch without breaking her fingers and skin a rabbit before the water had time to boil, but what good was any of that out here? They had no firearms to win Kai back with brute force, nor precious goods to barter for his release. They only had a few blades, the ferocity of Gerda's devotion to Kai, and the strength of their affection for one another to protect them now.

Helvig tipped her chin up a few inches, pointing silently to the walk. For a long moment, there was nothing, and Helvig's protective grip on Gerda's arm began to slacken.

"I thought I saw..."

A metallic voice rang out from behind them, and every muscle in Helvig's body stiffened.

"What is this?"

Gerda gasped and spun around, but Helvig was frozen in place. The world around her slowed to a crawl. Her chest seized so tightly it pained her, and fear beyond anything she had ever experienced was squeezing her heart.

Impossible. It was impossible.

She felt that if she lost her nerve right then and crumpled unconscious into the snow, she may never wake up again.

Helvig turned around.

Astrid stood before her, terribly tall and terribly real with a beauty that burned like frostbite. Her once plump cheeks were starvation-hollow, and fractals of ice and tattered mist-gauze clung to a frame that had wasted away to almost nothing. Her skin had the grey cast of the dead and was pulled too tightly over cavernous collarbones and the jutting tendons of her thin hands. Her eyes were colorless mirrors.

Helvig gripped her knife with shaking hands. It seemed stupid now, to think that a bit of sharp metal would be of any use against a thing so absolutely alien. This wasn't a rabbit she could gut over her knee, this was memory entombed in blue-white flesh, her own nightmare sprung to life.

Gerda swayed in front of Helvig, and for a moment the thief worried she may swoon from terror or drop to her knees in supplication. But then Gerda pulled her spine straight as a sword and said,

"We seek the queen at the top of the world."

Her voice did not waver. How long she had practiced saying that in her head?

The creature, neither woman nor ghost, tilted its head at her like an animal appraising prey.

"There is no queen here. No kings. No priests. Only me."

That sound like teeth dragging across ice was her voice, human words straining through vocal cords that were no longer fit for the task.

Helvig wanted to do something, to scream or cry or grab Gerda by the hand and drag her out of this godforsaken place. But she could only stare, the guilt she had carried for so long sitting inside her like lead.

Gerda took a step forward, her voice ringing through the empty space.

"Three years ago, you took someone from me. I have travelled the length of this country to get him back. Where is my brother?"

The Snow Queen turned her head one way and then the other, quasi-transparent tendrils of hair swirling weightless around her face. It could have once been Astrid's honey-gold color, but was now so thin and pale that there was hardly any color in it at all.

"I demand to know what you've done with him," Gerda pressed on. "His name was Kai, he was just eleven years old when you let him tie himself to your sleigh, and you never brought him back. He has my hair and brown eyes, and he loves reading ghost stories and playing with jacks, and…"

Her voice broke, and the little hiccup freed Helvig from her catatonic distress. No matter how her mind raced, she had to resist panic. Gerda needed her, and so would Kai, if he was anywhere to be found.

Helvig came up behind Gerda, one hand on her shoulder,

the other gripping her knife. She wanted to be more comforting, but the eyes that had once belonged to Astrid were burning a hole in her forehead and robbing her of her strength.

"Gerda," she murmured.

"What have you done with him? *Where is my brother?*"

"Gerda," Helvig said, a little more firmly. She swallowed. "That's Astrid."

Gerda swiveled to stare at Helvig.

"Your old sweetheart?"

Memories flashed through Helvig's mind, of stealing a whole basket of hot biscuits from the bakery and sprinting across town to share them with Astrid before they cooled. They were an apology, for slipping in through Astrid's bedroom window a half-hour later than she had promised to the night before. She had been pinched for that, and berated until her ears burned, but when she presented her peace offering to Astrid, Astrid had laughed and kissed the sweet honey glaze from her fingers.

"Yes. No. I-I don't know," Helvig stammered, long-buried recollections flooding back into her mind. God, they had been so young, and Astrid had touched her so sweetly during those furtive hours they had stolen in the apple orchards. But then the arguing had started, and the accusations. The last time Helvig had seen Astrid, Astrid had been cursing a blue streak while her father dragged Helvig by her hair down the stairs of their home. "I don't think she recognizes me."

The Snow Queen stared through them, her feet leaving patterns of ice where they touched the ground. Bare feet, with overgrown nails and purplish veins. There was no way she could survive these conditions, but here she was, hovering on the brink of life and death with old magic holding her upright.

Some of the rage had left Gerda, and now she gazed at Helvig with her lips parted in dismay.

"Oh God, Helvig. Are you sure?"

"I would know her in my sleep."

And she had, hadn't she? Hadn't she suffered awful nightmares of a monster that wore Astrid's face, and thought it a product of her addled mind?

I should have paid attention, she thought. *I should have known.*

Shock filtered through Gerda's features, and then numb, nameless distress. All of the fight had gone out of her, and she looked very small facing down Astrid's stately, if grotesquely thin, figure.

"Let me try," Helvig said, and stepped in front of Gerda.

She raised her hands up in what she hoped was a friendly, non-threatening gesture, despite the knife she still clutched point-down.

"We don't want trouble. We just want the boy."

The Snow Queen blinked with lashes long enough to trap a passing fly.

"Boy?"

Helvig took a wary step forward, ignoring the way Gerda snatched for her sleeve to pull her back

"Yes, the boy. We're looking for the children they say you've taken. Where are they?"

The creature pursed her lips while she thought. It was a gesture Helvig recognized from when Astrid was alive, when she was herself and not this revenant.

Another wave of anguish hit, so big it almost took Helvig's knees out from under her.

"Children? No, I don't have any children. Not anymore."

She felt like she might be torn in two if she had to stand between Gerda and the Queen much longer.

"What about the ones you…" *Stole.* Helvig was very aware that those nails, so much like talons, could open her throat with a single flick. "Found. Don't you remember a little boy in the town square in Copenhagen? You took him into your sled. Please. Try and remember."

A slow smile spread across the creature's face, and Helvig suppressed a shudder.

"Oh, yes. So sweet. So clever and talkative. I remember him."

Gerda strained forward, but Helvig pressed her back. She didn't know everything Gerda was capable of, or what she may do now to endanger either of them. As it was, their well-being felt like a thread stretched tight enough to snap.

"What have you done with him?"

"Kept him. Loved him. Brought him here so I can look at him always, and never be without him."

"Then where *is* he?"

The creature spread skeletal hands in front of her as though the answer were obvious.

"With all of them. Safe, below the ground."

Helvig blinked. *Below the ground?*

Her mind raced, trying to solve the riddle.

Did that mean…dead?

Gerda made an awful noise, and Helvig turned just in time to see her crumple to the ground.

Gerda tangled her fingers in her hair and screamed and screamed until there was no air left in her lungs. Then she folded over, pressing elbows and forehead to the ice, and let sobs wrack her body.

A lump rose in Helvig's throat, one she hadn't been expecting. In her time with Gerda she had come to care for Kai in her own way, as a beloved shadow in Gerda's mind. But there was no time for mourning.

They needed to get out while they still could. Helvig had to pick up Gerda and convince her that it was worth it to go on living, that she could not give up and die in this God-forsaken place when they had only just met.

Helvig began to back away from the dead thing that wore Astrid's face, and then she stopped. An idea coursed through her like lightning.

Below the ground.

Helvig swept a foot across the frozen lake, disturbing the snow. The creature watched her silently, raising the hairs on the back of Helvig's neck, but she worked diligently to clear the snow while Gerda shouted Kai's name.

Beneath the layer of white, the ice was thick and partially

opaque. But she could still see the unmistakable shape of a human hand drifting up towards the surface, captured in perpetuity.

"Christ's blood," Helvig breathed.

She swept away a wider path of snow, sending flurries whirling up towards the sky. She must have looked ridiculous, but she kept on clearing snow and peering through dark waters until she found a swirl of black hair wrapped around a face in silhouette. A child. A girl.

"Gerda," she hissed. "Look."

Gerda pulled her reddened face up off the ground. She looked half-tethered to reality, but her eyes followed Helvig's gaze.

Gerda gasped.

In an instant she had lost all interest in the Snow Queen, and she was back on her feet, her breath coming in heavy white puffs. She ran to and fro across the ice, sweeping snow away with the hems of her skirts and stooping to clear it with the flat of her palms. Helvig wanted to help her but didn't feel comfortable turning her back on what was left of Astrid.

The creature watched Gerda with a curious hunger, touching the tips of her claws to the pads of her fingers. Just as Helvig was about to suggest they get out of there while they still could, Gerda cried,

"Kai!"

Gerda fell to her knees on the ice and began furiously sweeping away snow. A face emerged beneath the glassy sheen, pale-haired as Gerda with a young boy's apple cheeks. He was suspended on his back, one arm stretched over his head, legs curling down into the murky water. He looked as though he were only sleeping.

Gerda pressed fingers against her brother's mouth through the ice and let out a keening cry. Of agony or relief, it was impossible to say.

"Oh," the monster said softly, like she was watching a peach and violet sunset and not the unmaking of a young girl.

Gerda clawed frantically at the ground, leaving little

streaks of red on the ice. After a moment, she remembered she still had her knife, and she began stabbing at the barrier that separated her from Kai. Tiny flakes of ice flew up and into her hair. She was rambling in Danish. A prayer, perhaps, or a curse.

The Snow Queen began to drift closer to the siblings, macabre curiosity scrawled across her face. Helvig sheathed her knife and sprang between them, holding up her palms. Her heart felt like it was going to burst out of her chest, but she had to buy Gerda time however possible.

Helvig ran her tongue over cracked lips and summoned all the courage she had.

"Astrid." The word fell heavy from her lips, and it was a struggle to keep the fear out of her voice. She knew animals could smell it. Maybe ghosts could sense it too. Her breath was ragged. She wasn't ready to do this. "Astrid, little sparrow, it's me. It's Helvig."

The terrible face turned towards her, studying. They were so close that two steps would close the distance between them. Did this creature even have access to memories of Astrid's life on Earth? Helvig couldn't be sure, and she didn't know if she really wanted to find out.

"The highwayman's daughter," the creature pronounced carefully. Strange light flashed in those colorless eyes.

"Yes, yes!" Helvig grasped at their tenuous connection to each other. "I told you stories! I called myself a princess, remember? Princess of Thieves."

Astrid—for now she looked much more like the girl Helvig had snuck through windows to kiss—drifted closer. Helvig could not be sure her feet were really touching the ground.

"Helvig," Astrid said, slow and soft.

A hand tipped with fingernails like talons reached for her face, and it took every ounce of will in Helvig's body not to shrink back. She steeled herself and didn't shudder when those nails scraped over her cheek.

"You came back," Astrid said. Helvig could have burst

into tears. None of this was fair. She should never have to see Astrid again, and certainly not like this, an undying thrall of winter with bones so thin a fall might break them. She should never have to suffer watching Astrid's dead face twinge with false hope.

The walls of the fort, so wide and spacious only seconds before, felt like they were pressing in around her. She couldn't live through this moment again, couldn't survive having something torn out of her when she told Astrid that she could not stay, could not save her.

"I came for the boy, little sparrow," she forced out. Tears swam in her vision. "You're not well."

Another hand, colder than Helvig thought possible, came up to cup her face.

"I've missed you so much. Pretty Helvig. So alive."

"Yes, I'm alive, but I'm afraid…I'm afraid that you aren't. Not in the way you were."

Helvig's cheeks ached from the frigid touch. Whatever Astrid had become neither breathed nor blinked, just regarded her with glassy eyes.

"Stay with me," it cooed. "I'll put you under the ground and have you with me always."

Helvig shook her head, slowly at first and then faster when she realized she could not break away. The grip on her face tightened painfully.

It isn't her, Helvig urged herself, forcing the realization no matter how much it hurt. *Astrid died in that ice storm. This is nothing but a vessel with a few of Astrid's memories.*

"I cannot. We're taking the boy. Let him go." Then, with more force, "Let me go, Astrid."

The Snow Queen dragged her closer until her body was a ribbon of frost against Helvig's stomach and chest. The robber convulsed involuntarily. If Astrid didn't let go soon, Helvig would go into shock from the cold.

"Stay," Astrid ordered. She gripped Helvig's face so tight the tip of her nails drew blood, and pulled her in for a kiss.

"*Let me go!*"

Helvig didn't realize she was shouting until she heard her voice echo off the walls. Years of buried anger came bubbling up the surface and she thrashed against Astrid, the way she should have when Astrid had dragged her through her window and ordered her to stay with her always. The Snow Queen's face was a rictus of hatred, teeth thin and sharp as needles bared.

Gerda was shouting, but Helvig couldn't hear anything. The first time she and Astrid had parted ways, it had haunted Helvig for years. This time, it would happen the way she chose, and she would not live to regret failing to try and save herself.

Helvig writhed like an eel on a hook, nearly breaking the creature's grasp, but then she was thrown down onto the ground, hard.

Her face throbbed where it was pressed against gritty ice. She barely had time to catch her breath before the Snow Queen dragged her up again by the collar of her shirt.

Helvig's ribs seared with pain. A fracture maybe, or bruising so deep it purpled the bone. Fingers cinched around her throat and hoisted her up onto her tiptoes. Helvig wheezed and scratched uselessly at the death grip.

She was being suffocated in a grimy tangle of hair, pressed spine-creakingly tight to Astrid's chest. She would kill her like this, crushing her to death with her love. Black spots swam in Helvig's vision.

"STOP!" Gerda yelled, louder than the roar of blood in Helvig's ears. There was a dark cast to her voice that could only be a witch's command. "Take me!"

The creature did not release her vise grip on Helvig's throat, but she turned her face towards the witch.

"Gerda!" Helvig snarled. Her fear took the shape of anger, otherwise it would have crippled her, but one word was all she could manage with the life being choked out of her.

"I summon the spirits of this land, and of the water and sky," Gerda pronounced, voice strong even though she had screamed it to tatters. She was on her feet, standing over her brother's frozen body with fists clenched and her face tipped up at the sky. Blue only moments ago, it was now covered over with fast-moving grey clouds. "I invoke you, winter! I welcome your embrace! Take mercy on me in my misery and deliver me from this torment!"

Helvig was dropped unceremoniously back onto the ice. She wheezed and blinked as Gerda's face came into focus. Church bells rang in her ears.

Ther revenant glided towards Gerda, but the witch continued her invocation with tears freezing on her cheeks.

"I'm willing; take me! You can take this body for your own ends and I will serve you well, I swear on my blood. Only give me power over the ice so I can save the ones I love. This is all I ask in exchange for my life!"

Gusts of wind gathered themselves into a dervish around Gerda's feet, catching her long hair up in a vortex. She looked half-possessed.

God in heaven, she meant to make a deal with them.

"Gerda," Helvig rasped, slipping on the ice as she tried to pull herself back up. "Don't."

Overhead, the clouds roiled into a darker shade of gunmetal. Gerda was still shouting, daring nature itself to take her into its frigid embrace, and the Snow Queen shrieked in rage. She batted away the chunks of ice and debris that flew out of the maelstrom and pressed in towards the witch, claws raised against the wind.

She would kill her, Helvig realized. She would slash open Gerda's chest and bleed her dry if it meant keeping her prizes safely below the ground.

Helvig was on her feet well before she was steady on them, moving out of wild terror.

The wind nearly knocked her backward, but she put her head down and pumped her burning legs until she made headway through the gale. A dislodged rock flying through the air clipped her shoulder hard enough to make her cry out, and she worried something inside her may have come loose, but she kept scrambling forward.

Astrid was mere feet away now, straining to grab a fistful of Gerda's hair, but Helvig was close behind.

She knew what she needed to do. Without thinking twice, she seized the narrow window she had been given to do it in.

Helvig used the last bit of energy within her to close the distance between her and the Snow Queen, nearly losing her footing on the ice. Her father's knife gleamed ready and willing in her trembling hand.

Helvig thrust the blade into Astrid's back, high on her spine. Her knife slid up to the hilt between muscle and bone.

I'm so sorry, little sparrow.

Astrid screamed loud enough to rattle what was left of the ceiling, wracked with excruciating pain even in her waking death. She clawed for the knife as she staggered backwards, but Helvig didn't let go, not even when she almost vomited up the fish soup from breakfast.

She could hardly see anything through the tears blurring her vision, but she wrapped both hands around the knife, took a shaky breath, and twisted until she heard the sickening snap of vertebrae.

Astrid, or whatever force had been animating Astrid's body, dropped like a sandbag and took Helvig down with her.

Helvig pushed the body away with a cry, kicking her feet against the ice to get further away from it. It fell lifeless onto its side, mirror-eyes open forever to the sky.

"Oh God," she gasped, sobs bubbling up in her throat. "Oh Christ."

But there was no time for tears. Gerda was still inside the whirlwind of snow, holding onto life and sanity by a thread. Helvig dug her fingernails into the ice and crawled forward on her hands and knees, unable to stand upright in such punishing winds. Every foot was slow-moving agony, and she could hardly see through her own burning tears, but eventually she reached the eye of the storm.

Gerda stood with her palms up to the sky, back arched so far that it looked like she may snap in two. Her long hair had come free from its plaits and whipped around her neck like a noose, and her eyes were rolled up so the whites showed.

Helvig shuddered, both from the cold that made her teeth chatter, and from how ghastly Gerda looked. The thief pulled herself upright, knees aching, and smeared the tears from her face.

There was no way to tell how long Gerda had until she was lost forever, or how Helvig could break an enchantment so ancient and powerful.

Spiderwebs of ice had started to form over Gerda's hands and face. Whatever Helvig was going to do, she needed to do it soon.

Squinting against the wind, Helvig took a few steps back and got a running start.

Helvig crashed bodily into Gerda and wrapped her arms tightly around her. They hit the ground with a bone-shaking crash.

Immediately, the eddy of snow broke apart, tendrils ripping away from the spiral to lash out in all directions. Gerda convulsed gently on the ground, her eyes still rolled into the back of her head.

Helvig was terrified that she had been concussed, but with dangerously high winds and razor-sharp fractals of ice spinning through the air, all she could do was pull Gerda close and hold her through the storm. Helvig's ribs and shoulder screamed out for a doctor, but the only one available was unconscious in her arms.

"Come on," Helvig said. She patted Gerda's face briskly, willing color back into those bluish cheeks. The winds around them were dying down now, but the cold had settled deep into her aching bones. "Wake up, love. Please, Gerda. Come back to yourself."

She kissed Gerda's temple, cold as a slab of granite, and then pressed their foreheads together. The convulsions were farther apart now, perhaps one every three or four seconds, but there was still no evidence of vital life in her.

The roar of wind died down until the only gusts blowing through the hall were the irregular northern winds that tugged at Helvig's clothes.

"Helvig?"

Gerda's voice was weak, but she was alive. Helvig burst into delirious laughter, cradling Gerda's face in her hands. Gerda's eyes were her own, and a tiny bloom of pink was on her lips. Helvig kissed that bloom so delicately, and wiped long, wet strands of hair away from Gerda's face.

"You gave me such a fright. I really thought you were gone. What were you *thinking*?"

"I'm sorry," Gerda rasped, hooking a heavy arm around Helvig's neck. She took a few deep breaths, and her free hand spread against the ice at her side, searching for Kai. "She was going to kill you. She wasn't going to let him go. I had to keep you both safe."

"Sweet, foolhardy girl. When will you learn that you're of as much value as anyone else? You had that planned? All along?"

Gerda shook her head and attempted a weak smile. It looked like it caused her pain.

"Only in case of an emergency."

Helvig cracked an unsteady smile.

"And here I thought you were just going to ask nicely."

Gerda spied the body laying in a heap a few feet away, and her eyes widened. "Did I…?"

"No. She went after you, and I—"

Her throat tightened, refusing to let any more explanations pass. Gerda slipped her cold fingers into Helvig's tangle of hair.

"I'm so sorry," she murmured.

Then Gerda rolled onto her side and smoothed her fingers over the glistening death mask of her brother's face. She curled up beside him, pressed her lips to the ice, and shivered.

Helvig burrowed beside her, arms wrapped so tightly around Gerda that they ached.

"It should have never happened like this," Gerda said hoarsely.

Helvig kissed her shoulder. She felt like she could sleep for a thousand years and still wake up exhausted.

An eerie creak went through the fortress hall, and then another. It sounded like leather straining tight enough to snap, or a fir bending dangerously far in a windstorm.

Gerda and Helvig exchanged expressions of consternation.

"What was that?" Helvig whispered.

The ice underneath them bowed, and a crack split the air.

FIFTEEN

Gerda shot to her feet and pulled Helvig upright. The ground beneath their feet shuddered, the glossy surface sweating beads of water, and then split open. Helvig put her arms around Gerda's waist and hoisted her away from the faulty ice.

"Run!"

The frozen lake gave way beneath their feet faster than any natural thaw, hairline fractures bursting into gaping maws in the blink of an eye.

Behind them, the ice opened up under Astrid's body. The water swallowed her slowly, until even the last tendril of her hair had disappeared beneath the water.

When they had entered the room, it was impossible to say how deep the flood was. Now, as sheets of ice sloughed away and water poured out of the hall and back towards the lake, Helvig saw it could not have been more than ten feet or so. She and Gerda clung to pillars removed from the worst of it, but when water splashed over their feet, Helvig was surprised to find it was temperate, balmy even.

When Gerda saw how rapidly the flood was receding, she splashed back in to retrieve Kai's body, up to her hips in dark water

"You'll die of cold!" Helvig shouted, but the witch would not be deterred. She lunged around where she had last seen her brother, kicking up great splashes of water.

Her arms sliced through waves like knives, grasping for flesh and bone, and then, finally, she hoisted Kai's limp frame out of the water with both hands.

She sobbed aloud and pressed him to her chest, cradling him like he was still a baby. Helvig waded in after them both, knowing that it would take two people to carry his body out and give it a proper burial. The water was bathhouse-warm despite the frigid air, and steam curled up into the January sky. It was as though summer had come in a snap, but only to this one little piece of the world.

Then, to Helvig's amazement, Gerda started waving at her frantically.

"Helvig?" She sounded near hysterical. "Helvig, he's breathing!"

Gerda shook her brother and he retched up filmy viscous fluid. He gasped for breath, and Helvig's heart leapt into her mouth.

He had survived under the ice all this time? Did that mean—?

Water poured out of the hall, taking with it ice and debris and leaving behind the Snow Queen's most precious possessions. Children, dripping wet and bleary-eyed. Children who moaned foreign names and coughed up mouthfuls of lake water.

Helvig lurched forward, reaching blindly for the nearest form that appeared above the water. Fear for Gerda's life was replaced with a new terror, that these innocents would drown before she and Gerda could reach them all.

She dreaded brushing against Astrid's corpse, but the Snow Queen's body was nowhere to be found. It had vanished in the melt.

Helvig hoisted up the child nearest by onto her hip. A little girl, with color quickly returning to her cheeks and a tumble of black hair plastered against her head. Truly alive, not just animated as Astrid had been. She could not have been older than three.

A little boy staggered to his knees in the water, choking violently. Helvig grabbed him by the sleeve and hoisted him onto unsteady feet. He wobbled but stood, knobby kneed in summer breeches and an askew cotton cap. Older, maybe ten.

Helvig patted the life back into his cheeks.

"Can you breathe, boy? Can you see?"

The little girl clung silently to Helvig's neck, taking in the scene with round onyx eyes. The boy's coughing fit continued until he cleared the last of the water from his lungs. Then he scrubbed at his eyes with a wet hand and said in Swedish,

"Where is this? Where's my brother?"

The water was swirling around Helvig's ankles now, almost drained and forgotten. The receding tide revealed a smaller boy lying a few yards off. His nut-brown skin matched the boy in Helvig's grasp.

"Nils!" The bigger boy cried, and sloshed off to aid his baby brother. To Helvig's relief, the smaller one was alive too, and promptly started to cry.

Helvig left them to their hugging and hurried over to Gerda. She was seated on the ground with Kai pulled into her lap, and he held her tightly while she buried her face in his neck.

"Kai, Kai, my dear heart, I have been looking for you for so long! I knew you were alive. I knew it in my soul."

Three years beneath the ground. It didn't seem possible, but here he was, snub-nosed and freckled with eyes that were quick and intelligent despite his bewilderment.

"Gerda?" He managed.

Gerda continued to cover his face with kisses. Kai craned his neck up to take in the open roof and the imposing stone walls that enclosed them, blinking slowly.

"How did I get here? I don't remember...No, I remember

a sleigh. And a White Lady, just like in the stories." He looked back at his sister and seemed to truly see her for the first time. His brow furrowed, and he touched her face in wonder. "Gerda, why are you so big?"

Gerda's smile shattered, and her lips uselessly tried to form words adequate to explain what had happened. Helvig took a deep breath and put her hand on Kai's shoulder. It was plain to see that he had not aged in the long years Gerda had spent bloodying her feet trying to find him. He still wore the patterned knit sweater and the cuffed pants of a schoolboy not yet ready for a formal apprenticeship.

"I think..." Helvig began warily. "That you've lost some time. Three years, to be exact."

Kai squinted skeptically at her.

"And who are you?"

"Her name is Helvig and she is very dear to me," Gerda cut in. "And you will mind her as you would me."

"But what's going on?" Kai pressed, a bit of whine coming into his voice. Gerda had described him as having a scholastic bent, and now Helvig saw the scientist in him, unwilling to accept anything but the full and rational truth. "How did we come to be in this place? Where's mother? What city is this?"

The little girl clinging to Helvig's neck shivered. The cold was settling in again, only kept at bay for a short while by the miraculous thaw.

The Snow Queen may be gone, but winter remained, hungry and dispassionate.

Helvig gave Kai's shoulder a squeeze. "There'll be time for explanations later. Suffice to say we're friends, and you're a long way from home. It's important we get away from this place and start a fire before the cold creeps into your bones."

Gerda looked wrung-out, but she nodded. Even in this state, she was practical enough to recognize that their survival depended on finding shelter and drying their wet clothes.

Helvig put her free arm out for the brothers, who were loitering a few feet off with wide eyes. Nils, the little one, skittered over to the warmth of her body heat and curled his fingers into her sopping vest. His big brother followed, but warily.

"Please Ma'am, can Pettr and I go home?" Nils asked.

"Where's the other lady?" Pettr demanded, almost at the same time. His shifty eyes seemed to suspect that Helvig might put him right back under the ice at any moment.

Helvig glanced around the waterlogged hall, empty apart from the six of them. She opened her mouth, but then her chest caved in on itself and she closed it again. There wasn't enough strength in her yet to speak of what had happened.

"She's gone," Gerda said. Her gaze was fixed with concern on Helvig, but she made her voice bright for the sake of the children. "No more white witches to kiss the warmth out of you and put you under the ice, I promise. She can't get you anymore."

Gerda pulled herself to her feet, tugging Kai up after her, and put one arm around Helvig's neck while she clung to her brother's with the other.

They must have all cut a funny picture, two adolescent girls, a boy, and three children all clinging to each other with scarce family resemblance to pass between them. Still, the duties and anxieties of heading a family had been foisted upon Helvig without notice. It was like she had aged a decade in the last hour.

Helvig did not know whether there had been more children taken over the years. All she was sure of was the four live children huddling around her, chattering their teeth and asking for their mothers. Four children that needed her to keep them alive as long as it took to get back to Rávdná's, and with only a few scant hours of daylight left.

Helvig took a deep breath. Her heart ached, her shoulder screamed out for attention, and her skin burned where the cold air touched it, but she could be strong for a few hours more.

"Come on, then," she said to the little girl with her face buried in her neck. "Let's go untie the animals and get some color into those cheeks with a walk, and then we'll have a cozy fire and maybe a bit of bread. How does that sound?"

The children muttered their half-hearted agreement, not having much of a choice in the matter. Gerda's nod was more decisive. She had wiped her face clean of tears and was wearing her determined, unbothered mask. But a new light shone in her eyes whenever she looked at her brother.

"A perfect idea. Helvig, that little thing seems very attached to you. Are you willing to carry her?"

Helvig shifted the baby on her hip and winced when her shoulder barked.

"Are you hurt?" Gerda asked. Her fair brows knit together in distress, and she pressed closer to Helvig.

Helvig swallowed and shook her head tightly.

"You can have a look later. She's light, I'll manage. I'm afraid to put her down in the snow. Will you two take the boys?"

Gerda crouched down in front of the brothers. Nils stared at her wonderingly while Pettr stuck his fingers into the straps of his overalls and scowled like she was trying to sell him a dry milking cow.

"Nils and Pettr are your names, is that right?"

Pettr gave a nod. Seeing that he was going to be the more difficult one to convince, Gerda smiled at him. It was a lovely smile, one that could get Helvig to turn over her innermost thoughts at a moment's notice.

"And Pettr, what do you like? What is your most favorite thing to do?"

He eyed her up and down, trying to decide if she was made of the same stuff as the Snow Queen.

"Well…I like sweets. I like to eat them, and soft rolls and meatballs, sometimes."

Gerda twittered in delight.

"Good, good! What else?"

"Um…" Pettr twisted his overall straps. "I like to go see the boats with my papa at the harbor. He let me ride 'round the wharf on one, and I met the captain."

Gerda cast a knowing glance over her shoulder to her

brother and indicated him to Pettr with a nod.

"Well, it just so happens that my brother is a very fine sailor, and we used to live in a house right over a canal. We would sit up on our beds and wave out the window to the boats every morning."

Pettr's eyes lit up. "Really?"

"I swear it. Would you like to walk with us and ask my brother about the boats? I'm sure he has many fine sailing stories to share."

Kai caught on to Gerda's game and gave an enthusiastic nod, beckoning Pettr over.

"It's true! Why don't you bring your brother over and we'll talk man-to-man about it? You can tell me all about the ship you and your papa visited."

This won him. Pettr obediently fell into step with Kai, ushering his baby brother along and babbling about how unsteady on his feet he had been on the big ship. Within minutes they were all on their way in a tight formation, leaving the bitterness and the gloom of the great hall behind. Gerda and Kai walked with their fingers tightly entwined ahead of the pack, leading them through the dim corridors to a kinder world outside.

Helvig watched them with a deep sense of both elation and grief, the sort of feeling that could only accompany a satisfying ending to a beloved bedtime story. But this was not a story, she reminded herself, and if it was, it wouldn't be Helvig's — it would be Gerda's and Kai's, and this would be the moment Helvig faded back into the scenery while Gerda and Kai took center stage for their well-earned bows.

Light stung Helvig's eyes as they emerged from the fort, dazzlingly reflected off the white snow even as the sun sunk lower in the sky. The winds outside were harsh and unwelcoming, but Helvig was grateful to be back in the open under sun and sky again.

She hitched the small girl higher up on her hip and wrapped the babe's face in the scarf from her own neck. None of the boys were dressed for the weather, but Gerda held them close and gave Kai her gloves, which was all she had to spare.

They would make it. They had to.

Kai cast a wary glance to Helvig. He wasn't stupid. He must know their odds. Helvig nodded to him grimly.

"Look!" Gerda said.

Two dark figures had arisen over the horizon of one of the hills that blocked their way back to Rávdná's camp. Gerda stepped in front of Nils and Pettr, shielding them with her body as best she could.

"Who is that?" Helvig asked, squinting against the sun.

"No more thralls I hope, or spirits. I've had my fill of that."

"Looks like people to me," Kai said.

A third figure climbed over the horizon, and then a fourth and a fifth. One of them rode a stocky black horse, and another led a reindeer laden with packs and pouches.

"Oh no," Helvig said.

Gerda took a few steps forward, shielding her eyes from the glare.

"Is that...your father?"

"I'm going to get the scolding of my life."

Berthold plodded along on the black mount with two of his men following on foot and Rávdná leading the deer behind. Rasmus trudged in the snow beside her father, his hands bound and tied to Berthold's saddle. Had he dragged Rasmus like that the whole way?

"Rasmus!" She shouted. The was no need to worry about not being spied by the rescue party, as it was probably difficult to miss six children standing in a clump near an abandoned fort. She mostly just needed to shout, out of relief or anger or fear or any of the other emotions that had been swirling around inside her all day.

"Sorry, Helvig!" Rasmus shouted back across the plain. He skittered down the snowy slope and jogged to keep pace with the horse. Helvig resolved to make this up to him with an all-expenses paid trip to the pub and maybe a new jacket with shining buttons.

It took a few nerve-wracking minutes for the two parties to cross the plain to one another. Helvig wondered how she could possibly explain running off to her father, or if there was any way she could clear Rasmus of further culpability. Explanations of dire need and defenses of rash actions flickered through her head, presenting themselves like faces on a die.

But when Helvig finally stopped in front of her father's huge horse, shivering and holding up the weight of a strange child, she found she didn't have anything to say.

The Robber Kind swung off his horse, his mouth set into a ferocious scowl.

"I'm sorry, papa," Helvig said, meek for once in her life. Tears stung her eyes.

Berthold crushed his daughter into a bear hug. Helvig, to her embarrassment, cried into her father's chest in front of Rasmus and Gerda and everyone else. She buried her face in his coat and breathed in his familiar scent of leather and pipe smoke and cried until she was dry.

"I'm so cross with you," Berthold said, his own voice thick with emotion. "But I'm so glad you're alive. Rasmus said you had gone to see your god-aunt and I didn't know if you would make it, in this weather."

Rávdná gave Helvig a look that said *I know better than you and I'm not sorry about it.* Helvig couldn't be upset with her, though. Rávdná was a businesswoman before anything else and it would have been terrible for trade if she harbored a regular customer's fugitive daughter and sent her off into the wilderness without aid.

Helvig tried on one of her cocky smiles, even though her face was still wet.

"You should have trusted your own raising. We were fine, papa, really."

Berthold smoothed his daughter's hair with his massive hands. He always touched her like a diamond set into delicate filigree, or a purse that needed extra light handling to filch.

"For God's sake, what are you doing out here at some abandoned old fort? Rávdná said you were looking for ghosts." He nodded to the child clinging to Helvig's neck. "And who are these children?"

Helvig pressed her cheek against the little girl's and gave her father the same smile that had won her Bae so many years ago.

"We found them. They have no one. We had to take them with us; they would have died out here alone."

Gerda stepped forward, one arm slung around her little brother to keep him warm. She bobbed a curtsy, elegant despite the number of near-death experiences she had gone through over the last few days.

"Your Majesty, I would like to present my brother, Kai, long a prisoner of the Snow Queen."

Berthold blinked at the siblings and then shook his head. He took one of Gerda's thin shoulders in his hands and pointed a finger into her face. Not to threaten, merely to emphasize.

"I don't know what you really are, little witch, but this is madness. It's simply too much." He waved at his men to gather the stolen horse. Helvig allowed it, but loitered territorially near Bae. "Come on, all of you. Let's get away from this eerie place and get a fire going and then you'll all be telling your tales, one by one in an orderly fashion. I can't believe you've got some kind of fairy tale circus going on out here in the middle of nowhere, Helvig."

Gerda chattered her part of the story as they began their chilly trek towards safer ground. The king listened with rapt incredulity, sometimes shaking his head despite the evidence strolling beside him in the form of a very confused Danish boy.

Helvig drifted over to Rasmus and began to untangle the knots around his wrists with her fingers and teeth. It was awkward work with a child clinging to her, but Rasmus helped the best he could.

"I'm sorry about this," Helvig said. A month ago,

apologizing to one of her men would have hurt like pulling teeth. Now, culpability came easy. "You shouldn't have gotten in trouble for me. I'll tell him so."

Rasmus massaged the blood back into his wrists. There were dark circles around his eyes from a sleepless night on the road, but he didn't look much worse for wear otherwise. "It's alright. Happens to the best of us sometimes."

"He wallop you?"

"Not badly. He knows I can't take much."

"Old man's going soft," Helvig scoffed, but she couldn't help putting an arm around Rasmus' shoulder and pulling him in tightly.

In the past she would have never wanted to give him the idea that they were so familiar, that perhaps underneath her tough exterior she felt some genuine affection for him. Now the bravado seemed stupid, and she was just grateful to have someone who knew her at her worst and still wanted to play cards with her, or go out foraging together, or listen to her ramble on about whatever was eating her up inside.

"Looks like you are too," Rasmus ribbed, but he put both arms around her and tucked his face into her neck in a proper hug. "You owe me."

Helvig squeezed the back of his neck to show that she understood, and that she swore on thieves' honor to pay him full recompense.

Rasmus straightened and sniffed, hunching his shoulders forward as though embarrassed.

"Not so bad, getting out of camp," he said, all bluster again. "Nice scenery. Fine clear air. And I saw a real bear, too. Walked right up to me. I touched its coal-black nose."

"Course you did. Did it hop on its hind legs and dance for you too?"

Rasmus deftly changed the subject by jutting his chin out at the child on Helvig's hip. It seemed like he wanted to reach out and touch it but wasn't quite sure how.

"You found.... a baby?"

Helvig fell into step behind him as they started their long

walk back up the hillside and towards the safety of the Sami camp.

"She's in fine health, too. Won't Wilhelm be thrilled? Finally, he'll have a little thing to catechize and teach German to, and he'll leave us alone about it."

"I'll praise God for that. How'd you come into possession of such a gem?"

Helvig glanced back at Gerda. The witch had somehow charmed Berthold so much that he was allowing her to walk with one arm threaded through his elbow and another one threaded through Kai's. Probably by asking nicely.

"It's a very long story, but I'll tell it if you feel like listening. In the meantime, how do you feel about a new sister?"

SIXTEEN

Despite her embarrassment about being hunted down like a lost sheep, Helvig was grateful for her father's presence. He had more experience warding off cold than she did, and he showed them all how to slowly warm the blood so as to preserve their own body heat and prevent shock.

The children recovered quickly despite being kept under a spell for so long. Soon the girl Helvig had rescued regained her powers of babbling speech, and the pair of boys put away more of the venison and biscuits that Rávdná had brought than Helvig thought their stomachs could hold. They talked tirelessly between bites, telling stories of their parents and their schoolmates and how they had been tempted away into the forest one evening by a beautiful woman who offered them candied fruits and chocolates. Gerda supplied what answers she could, huddled next to Kai close to the fire, and Rávdná interjected with certain sightings that suggested the Snow Queen was more than a fable.

Once they were stable enough to keep moving, the King ordered them to pack up camp and press on for the Sami village, where they would spend a night safe and among friends. By this time, he had forgiven Rasmus for failing to guard the horses and for helping Helvig run away, and he gave the boy a light load to carry on the walk. Once again the only two people of their age in the band who were not otherwise diverted with long-lost relatives, Helvig and Rasmus walked in time together, telling tall tales to keep themselves warm.

Helvig collapsed as soon as she was back to the *lavvu* and slept more soundly than she had for weeks, close to Gerda and Kai with her newest little friend asleep on her stomach. She supposed the girl had gone under the ice before she had learned how to speak, and so Helvig took it upon herself to give her a name. Never the poet, she settled on January, for the month in which she had been found.

"Such big eyes," Kai had commented drowsily as they settled in to sleep. "She just keeps staring at everything."

Helvig chuckled, winding a finger around one of January's black ringlets. The babe was gazing at Kai with her thumb lodged in her rosebud mouth.

"S'pose there's a lot to look at after behind under ice for years and years," Helvig said. A dull ache still throbbed through her shoulder where Gerda had tightly wrapped it. She had assured Helvig that nothing has been permanently damaged or knocked out of place so badly it needed realignment.

"That's for sure." Kai nestled down next to his sister, who had lovingly spread out blankets and furs for him the way she would for a small child. "Fresh air, warmth; I can't get enough of any of it. I feel like I could walk the world over and not get tired of seeing grass again, or horses, or clouds. I wouldn't mind seeing our old house again, either, or those little flowerboxes hung outside our bedroom window"

Gerda smoothed her brother's hair away from his face even though it wasn't mussed. She leapt at every opportunity to touch him, to remind herself he was real.

"I'll take you wherever you want to go. I promise you, we'll see Copenhagen again. Everyone will be overjoyed to see you back in the city, and they'll eat their words for thinking you dead."

Helvig let them reminisce until drowsiness demanded they put out the light. January's warm weight lulled Helvig into a stupor, but anxiety pricked at her mind while she drifted off to sleep. Though Gerda was close enough to touch, she felt miles out of reach, and like she was getting further away with every passing hour. Nothing felt fixed. Everything was transient, shifting like marsh grass that could swallow a traveler up if they weren't careful.

In the morning, they all began their trek back to the encampment where the King had left his men with strict orders not to kill anyone while he was gone. He had left a second-in-command in charge, and the brigands generally wanted to avoid outright civil war and so behaved when left alone for short periods of time. But Berthold was eager to reassert his presence as their leader. Rávdná sent Helvig off with kisses and a new knife set into a reindeer antler handle, and she gifted Gerda bright blue ribbons for her beautiful hair. She promised that the next time they three saw each other, it would be under happier circumstances. Helvig ached with the knowledge that in all probability, Gerda would not be returning to Rávdná's with her in the spring to do trade.

Gerda and Kai were inseparable, hardly ever letting each other go much less drifting out of reach. Helvig had never seen Gerda look so open to her own happiness, and every one of her radiant smiles brought a smile to Helvig's own lips while piercing her heart. All good things ended eventually, she reminded herself. Even if you could manage to keep someone at your side your whole life long, death would eventually part you. She should know better than to be upset.

Late into their journey home, when the snowy ground had become mottled with scrub and the horizon promised the secure embrace of evergreens, Gerda slipped away from Kai. She left him with Rasmus, who was telling one of his braggart's tale to wonderstruck Pettr, and fell into step alongside Helvig.

They were trying to spare the horse and Bae by letting them walk unburdened for a while, and so Gerda was able to slip her arm through Helvig's as they strolled.

"I can't thank you enough for coming with me," the witch

said. She was wearing her hair pulled back from her face with one of her blue Sami ribbons. "If I had gone up there alone and seen Kai like that...I thought I was ready to find his body, but I wasn't."

"I didn't feel very useful at the time, but you're welcome all the same."

They moved slowly over snow and grass, Gerda running her thumb in circles over Helvig's arm. Helvig tried to memorize the curve of her face, the bow of her lips, and the precise color of her hair so she could cherish these vestiges of Gerda when she was gone.

"You still blame yourself for what happened with Astrid?" The witch asked, in her unprompted, probing way.

Helvig sighed heavily. This close to the forest, she could smell the sharpness of birch and fir welcoming her home.

"I don't know. Every time I think about it, I remember it differently. I think...I don't know. I hope I was doing her a mercy, in the end."

Gerda's eyes skimmed the horizon as she nodded sagely.

"I think that's wise of you. Still, no matter how we feel about how it came to us, death is a thing to carry. I don't want you to feel like you have to carry it alone."

Helvig shrugged. She had carried Astrid's first death inside her for three years before Gerda had appeared to ease the weight. She would manage the weight of the second after Gerda had moved on.

"People die. It's just the way of things."

Gerda rested her chin on Helvig's shoulder.

"I'm so ready for this to be over. I'm so tired, Helvig. I feel like I haven't slept in years."

Helvig tried to smile, but it felt thin and brittle.

"Well soon you can be on your way with your brother, together at last. I'm sure your parents will be missing you."

Gerda's eyes were injured. "Oh. I didn't realize you wanted us to go so soon."

"No, no!" Helvig fumbled, nearly stopping in her tracks. The last thing she wanted was to push Gerda away any faster.

"Of course I don't want you to, it's just...You can't very well expect Kai to be happy to stay out here in the dirt with a bunch of criminals. And you..." Helvig caught her breath and reminded herself that they had already had this conversation ten times in her head. There was nothing to be afraid of, just a duty to perform. "I've held you here long enough. It was selfish of me, to try and stop you from getting your brother back."

"I thought I was your prize and your spoil," Gerda teased. "I was just starting to like being hoarded like crown jewels."

Helvig squeezed Gerda's hand and swallowed the last of her nerves. There was nothing left to lose now at the end of their journey, so she had better just come out and say it.

"I love you, Gerda. Ferociously and terribly, so much that it scares me. All you have to do is lift a finger and I would follow you to the end of the earth. But I cannot do to you what Astrid did to me, and if I force you to stay, I'll be just as bad as her. Loving something doesn't mean that you own it."

Gerda hummed thoughtfully, and the two of them continued in silence for some time. Behind them, the horse snorted and clopped while Berthold filled Kai in on what sort of wars Sweden had been embroiled in since he went under the ice, and how Denmark had fared in recent negotiations. The King loved to illuminate the ways of the world to an eager pupil, and Kai had been voraciously absorbing Berthold's lectures since returning to himself. Helvig could see how much he took after his sister in keen intelligence. January rode hoisted on the Robber King's back like a travel pack, screeching with incomprehensible delight at Bae, or the clouds, or a rock.

"Kai will need time to get re-acclimated to the world," Gerda said. "And he grew up on a steady diet of books about pirates, so I think he'll be more thrilled than you know to find himself in a den of thieves." She stopped to take a shaky breath and cast a wistful glance to her brother. "I'm not sure if there are parents to go home to, Helvig, or if they would know the people we've become after all these years. At any rate, we don't need to leave tomorrow, and maybe, when we go, we won't have to travel alone."

Helvig stopped and turned to examine Gerda's face. There was no falsehood in her, just pragmatism and an untested tenderness.

"What are you saying?"

Gerda wrung her hands. Nerves. "I won't ask you to go with us, it wouldn't be fair. You have responsibilities here, and a father who loves you, and men who need you. But after spending so much time in this world alone I'm afraid I've grown accustomed to having you at my side. More than that, you give me peace, and you make me think...You make me hope that perhaps I could fix whatever's broken inside me and learn to be more trusting, more warm..."

"Gerda, Gerda..." Helvig pressed the witch's hands between her own. "No, you're wonderful, there's nothing broken about you."

"There is no one I would rather walk the roads of this earth with, is all that I'm saying. You don't have to decide now, of course."

Hope, which Helvig was sure had laid down and died over the last two days, stirred inside her chest.

"And what if people talk about us? Call us improper?"

"I've never cared about being proper, and you and I both know there are things in this world more powerful and terrible than people's opinions. Your father doesn't seem to care, or your friends. Who else matters?"

Helvig's heart burned in her chest, and she felt drunk with possibility.

"It could be dangerous for the three of us out on the road together."

Gerda smiled. "If you haven't learned by now that I welcome danger as an old friend, you haven't learned very much about me."

-kai!

Helvig looked up to find a familiar black blur winging towards them from the trees, bands of gold glinting on its feet.

"Svíčka!" Gerda cried. Her crow alighted on her shoulder with a squawk, and she nuzzled its feathery head with her cheek.

"Tough old girl," Gerda said fondly. "She so hates to be left behind."

January clapped her hands at the arrival of the crow, trying to shape the word for "bird" with her hooting lips. The Robber King glanced over at the girls, heads close in lover's talk, and averted his eyes politely.

Helvig cupped Gerda's face and kissed her like an oath, the sensation spreading through her body with the slow surety of spring thaw. When she pulled away, her eyes shone with delight.

"I'll gladly take these things into my consideration. But tonight, we celebrate. For once in my life I've got a story better than Rasmus', one that really happened. And I intend to tell it for all it's worth with you at my side. That's if you'll deign to be kept for another night more, Miss Sorceress?"

A warm flush spread across Gerda's cheeks, pink as window box roses.

"Oh, I think we can manage one night more, at the very least."

ABOUT THE AUTHOR

S.T. Gibson is a poet, author, and village wise woman in training. By day she works for an audiobook publisher in New England and by night she retreats to her home to scribble speculative stories. You can connect with her on Twitter @s_t_gibson, on tumblr at stgibsonoffical.tumblr.com, or on her website stgibson.com.

Printed in Great Britain
by Amazon